Urma Applebaum and the Pigman

Rich Unkel

Saguaro Books, LLC
SB
Arizona

Cover Artist: Xander Smith
AFX Studio

Saguaro Books, LLC
16845 E. Avenue of the Fountains, Ste. 325
Fountain Hills, AZ 85268
www.saguarobooks.com

ISBN: 978-0-692-20351-4
Library of Congress Cataloging Number
LCCN: 2021932843
Printed in the United States of America
First Edition

Dedication

I dedicate this book to all my students, as they have taught me how to grow as a teacher.

Table of Contents

Prologue
My Ploy

I wish the drama in my life was normal but it isn't.

Catching you up to speed will not be speedy. With everything that's going on, I have a big decision ahead of me and I'm not sure what to do. In fact, I don't know what any 14-year-old girl would do in this situation.

I just turned 14, actually. I'm not trying to put myself down and say, "Well, I'm just a teen and I only know a little." Actually, I know too much. I should be enjoying life yet I am stuck in a dilemma. Is this what being a teen is all about? This is what I have to face right now? A major decision. A "what do I do?" or a "what would you do if you were in this predicament?"

This is a difficulty I didn't want to be in either. Aren't most crises like that? A lot of times we just ask what we should do when we already know what we want to do. This is different. I don't know what to do. I'm not even sure how to handle this situation.

So, if I ask you, "What should I do," I have to explain the complete mess and if I don't explain the entire story in the here and now, you won't understand the big picture. You need to understand it involves all that in this decision. Plus, you need to know all the people who are potentially affected in this dilemma to make a sound judgement.

Many times people want someone's opinion but then, they only receive a one-sentence explanation. This is a little different, a lot different, actually. There's so much to process right now. I think it would be better if I took you through the entire story so you and I could process this issue together.

You could help me make a better decision than the one I could make right now on my own.

Please bear with me as I take you through the total story.

Give me your undivided attention, please. It will only help me make a better decision. I'm kind of scaring myself right now because I'm sounding like my mother. Yes, I am laughing aloud as I am writing this.

So here it goes. Here is the entire story to bring you right to the present. I am on an island and I am not going anywhere soon. I feel as if I am stuck. Only an ocean of despair and let-downs surround me, a mixture of fear and conundrum, with a slice of depression.

I know too much.

It might take me awhile to tell you everything, though time is running out. I sort of need to decide soon. You will see my need to make the right decision. Here, the wrong decision could be detrimental; unfortunately, so could the right decision.

I don't want to leave anything out.

Also, I don't just ask people who I know will give me the answer I am looking for. You know what I am talking about. You want to hear a certain answer, therefore you ask the "right" friend to give you the "right" answer. I need more than that. This involves a lot of potentially hurtful information that could ruin people's lives.

It all started with this turn of events in my life.

I'm good at reading my mom's face while she's on the phone. If she rolls her eyes, it's probably grandma. I know if she writes notes that I probably have a dentist appointment coming up. When it's good news, her face transforms from a pensive look to an enormous smile. Those are easy to figure out but there's one look I've seen that I'll always remember. The look my mother gets when somebody calls with news, news that isn't good. We all know what the worst news is that one can get. Death.

If you've never dealt with death before, let me try to give you a brief glimpse of what it's like. It is so strange. It's so weird. It's this distinct feeling you can't really explain unless you've gone through it. The person is just not there anymore. They're gone. I've always gone to visit my grandmother. This time when we go there, she won't be home. There won't be anyone at her house, no one to greet us at the door. She vanished.

Yes, I know where she is and I know her whereabouts. It is just that she's not there. Not present with us anymore. I've never experienced this feeling of sadness that hits so hard then it kind of resurfaces at different times for different reasons.

Chapter 1
What I Am

I used to be embarrassed because when I see something messy, I have to organize it but I have realized through help with people explaining it to me, it is a talent. With any talent you don't let it get too far, meaning, make sure it is a healthy obsession. I'm sounding like my mother again but it is true. Sometimes I need to stop myself. I don't have to clean everything in this world. There are some things that are much better left messy.

That's why I always enjoyed visiting my grandmother. Sometimes I didn't realize it was maybe that it wasn't so much my grandmother and I were alike; it was just that my grandmother and I were both different from my mother. My mother is very straight laced and by the books and I am not as much, except for the organization part of course. My grandmother and I always want to question things. I guess we're somewhat inquisitive. Also, the two of us love to write. She is a pretty well-known writer in her little small Vermont town. I'm not as much known but I definitely help people at school with their school work and especially the writing. I just understand that stuff, plus I love to type things on my type reader and word process things. Writing is kind of my get away from it all and I know my grandmother feels the same way. So maybe we both write to get away from the rules of my mother. My mother is a wonderful mom, she's just different. Same in my grandmother she is much different from my mother and I guess if anybody, she's a little like me and I am a little like her. We were allies in a way. My mom differs from me and different still from my grandmother.

She had clutter; I guess for the right reasons. Her house was filled with things, many things. Each thing had a purpose and, if you asked her about a thing or an object, you would get a story behind it. Her house was filled with memories, stories and reminders.

Each time we visited, she had a room or area she would let me organize. I was in my glory. I would occasionally stop and ask her what the story was behind an object. From old books to dusty statues, her tales were usually lengthy and filled with a laugh or a tear. It seemed she would only keep things that had that effect. Makes sense, really.

She was our only family. Living way up in Vermont, we only saw her a couple times a year. One year we came here three times as my aunt had passed away. That was about four years ago, though.

Mom is an only child and my grandfather died in the Vietnam War. My grandfather was a young farmer drafted into war. He went. He served his country. Mom was sixteen months when it happened. Grandma never remarried. She remained married to her work. She was always busy and elbow deep in something. From church events to book clubs and town events, she was always on the go.

My grandmother's different-than-my-mother's ways made sense because she was the town historian so she had many objects in pictures, photos, drawings and artwork from local people, places, events and time periods from the past. She even had a little model of the town's Main Street that a local high school student locally had made for their senior project. It showed what the town looked like in the mid-1800s.

Going to Grandma's house was quite an event and I admit there were times I had to stop myself from scanning the room and doing an inventory of what I could clean and what I could organize. Instead, I would just slow down, stop and realize when people are different; it doesn't mean one person is better than the other. We are just different and being different is good. I'm glad my grandmother was how she was. It made her interesting. It made her life interesting. She taught me much.

Embracing each other's differences has helped me realize that my desire and passion to clean or organize is needed. Also, it is not needed and not to be spoken about. There is a time to talk and time to let silence speak for it.

In fact, one time we had a sleepover at Kristen's house. It was going well until popcorn was spilled everywhere. The entire bag emptied onto the floor and quickly got trampled. When we all watched Netflix out on the big screen, I stayed behind. Cleaning up mashed, buttery popcorn on a green carpet was more of a need than binge watching any show. A mess such as that was as serious as a burning building with children and animals trapped inside. Nothing else matters. Well, as you can tell, I spent most of the night absent from the group and present with the task at hand. When I finished cleaning, I realized Kristen's room was an unorganized heap of neediness, needing my personal touch and talents. Well, after everyone fell asleep, I did my work. As the tooth fairy, there was much change done when the girls awoke.

"Wow, Trinity…" They all said, in their own interpretations of the work completed while they lightly snored. I was rubbing the sleepy seeds from my eyes while they wanted me to go to their rooms and do the same thing.

"I'll do it during the day and not as an all-nighter instead of hanging with you," I declared.

They agreed.

I organized and they did the party thing. Organizing, well, that's my party.

I've also been hired by friends who are grounded and can't go anywhere until their room is clean. I've made much cash that way. When you do something such as that, news travels fast.

Even one of my friends' friend's mothers hired me to clean and organize. I charged her double as she had a job and I would not clean an entire house for a little hourly wage.

She lay on the couch. I cleaned. I am not sure what kind of deal it was for her but I was happy to help and collect my money.

At Christmas, I organize all the presents under the tree. There are areas for each person. When we sit down to open gifts, I take one from each pile and hand them out. I bet you can guess who has to have all the wrapping paper after each present is opened. Yep, I fold them all and put them in the large black trash bag I have next to my chair. They have called me the Grinch twice, so I have to not be so intense about it. I enjoy Christmas. I always do.

I am not a "neat-freak," if that is how you are pegging me. I just want organization. My stuff gets dusty. I keep up with it. That's normal.

There is one area of my life I guess you could call odd. I like computers, as I own one. I play video games and normal stuff on it; however, for typing, I like the old-fashioned typewriter. Kind of different, but I love them—the clicking of each letter hitting the paper on the roll. The ding it makes at the end of the line and I love the font. It is so cool and I want all my writing in that font. What I discovered is that some typewriters have a little different font. So, I can't have just one. Like pairs of shoes, I have many. Depending on the writing I do, I use different typewriters. I don't really know of anyone my age who has the same passion for old typewriters. Odd, but my odd. Cool, I love clicking away on my Olympia SM7. I am sure that you are not sure what I am talking about. The font is a diamond pitch size seventeen. I am confident I am not speaking your language. No worries. It's similar to a Courier font on Microsoft Word or Google Docs. Check it out.

I type my homework and research papers on the old school typewriter. My teachers think it is interesting that I have a love for the old typing machines—Mr. Edger, especially. He is my English teacher and always appreciates reading my work. He says it reminds him of when he was young and the days before computers ruled the world. I still love my phone and computer. He understands.

Cleaning and typewriters are simple. When you clean a room it is finished. It is complete and you can see the results of your hard work. It is satisfying because you know you can do it. It is freeing because it is much better than how you found it. Typewriters are simple, too. You use them as a tool and they help you accomplish a goal. They are nothing less than wonderful. What I need your help with, though, is complex. It is a big mess that I can't even tackle.

I don't have any friends who share my passions. I mean, who, at my age, has an obsession for organizing and typewriters? The good thing is it has driven no one away. My friends like that I have these differences. We all do, if we look close enough. That about sums me up.

Nobody likes to see their parents cry. It isn't fun. For me, because they are older it hurts us more to see them sad; probably because it happens so few times. Sure, there is crying when we're watching a movie together and there's a sad part. My mother's crying now is in the present reality. It is her sadness because of the loss of her mother. It will be like that one day for me when I lose her. I can't imagine that feeling. Everything you've known since you were a child is now gone—that foundation, that person who is always there, that person who always picks up when you call. That was my grandmother for my mother and that is my mother for me.

What an incredible void.

I'm sure my mother's void is even larger than mine.

I firmly believe part of my mother's sadness was she and her mother didn't get along and they probably should have. They didn't get along and my mother and I do. Pretty much. Sure, the reality of her mother not being there was deeply saddening because there was no time now to fix some things that had been slightly broken through the years. Like I said, we only went there a couple times a year and there were many reasons for that.

My mother and her mother did not see eye to eye. It took me years to figure that out, as my mother was always respectful of my grandmother. My grandmother was always nice to my mother but I knew there were some underlying things that didn't quite mesh. They didn't quite align in their views of things. What two people really align perfectly? I don't think that really exists but their differences were a little obvious. As time went on, I could gradually see where they did not see eye to eye.

My grandmother was always slightly resentful that my mother moved far away. My mother moved far away because of the career she wanted to pursue. It is somewhat hard to be a paleontologist way up in the vast wilderness of the Green Mountains of Vermont.

Then when my mother didn't end up being a paleontologist, for which she went to school, she never moved back to the area. She changed her career and became an x-ray technician at our local hospital. She went to night school while raising me. I've always had so much respect for my mother as she works hard. She and my grandmother are two different people. Unfortunately, I think my grandmother thought differences were slightly negative. When, for example, my mother quit college to get married (for five minutes before she divorced my father) and have me. My grandmother didn't take kindly to that. Then as I got older, she went back to school and started a career and grew deep roots where we live now, here in Pennsylvania. Hershey, Pennsylvania is a cool place and I absolutely love it here. Well, I don't know any different, really. It has everything I need and everything we need as a family. As my mom always says, "Why would we move away from the city of chocolate?" Mom and I have enjoyed living in a quiet little house in a quiet little neighborhood. I respect that my mom works hard 9 to 5, Monday through Friday. We usually spend our nights and weekends together. There is so much to do here and to explore.

As you can figure out, my dad isn't in the picture anymore. Actually, I've never met him. I have a few photos of him but they are old ones and he looks almost my age in them. As my mom will say, “the pregnancy lasted longer than the marriage.” She has made that comment a few times through the years. “We are blessed,” she will always reply when she makes any comment about my biological father. She’ll always remind me, “You and I are family, Trin,” and she will never say anything mean about him. “It just didn’t work out and that’s OK as we have each other and I will love you forever,” She says, often trying to make it rhyme. That’s good enough for me and I don’t pry for more information. I don’t desire to see him either.

I will go to attend private high school next year and I’m a little nervous about that. It seems as this spring break will be taken up by me and my mom going to clean out my grandmother’s house right after we complete all the plans for the funeral. I don’t think it’s what she wants to be doing all summer but as she says, “We have no choice and we must go.”

Chapter 2

Newbie in Town

Mom and I have always lived here in Hershey.

It has always been our home.

Hershey, Pennsylvania, has something like 14,000 people living there. To me, it's a small city. A perfect size city with everything I need. Northfield, Vermont, not so much. We come here every summer for about two days and sometimes for Christmas or Easter. So I've seen enough of the town to know all about it. I know there's less than half a population of Hershey. So to me that makes this town less than 50 percent exciting.

Now, we are here trying to make sense of my grandmother's death. I am trying to make sense of my mother, trying to make sense of her mother's death. Our new normal, I guess.

The greatest part about being here is that there's literally no data coverage on my cell phone. Obviously I am being facetious. Hate it. Lothe it. Tired of it. Within minutes, I wanted to leave. Who would want to be here? It is like when the power goes out. You realize how many conveniences we rely upon. Trust me, the power is completely out here. In this town and at my grandmother's house, there is no Verizon coverage at all. Luckily, my grandmother has the internet here at her house. She was constantly online researching things. She had a strong online presence in her community and beyond.

There is a military college here, but I really literally know nothing about it. I don't know anybody, anyone who's gone to it. My mother grew up here and does not know anybody, anyone that went to Norwich University. The campus is beautiful and we've walked through it a few times.

There are some town shops and thrift stores that are somewhat cool and there are antique stores where last summer I bought a typewriter. I believe it was a little overpriced but I talked the store owner down to a decent amount.

I'm literally getting bored just explaining this town to you. There is nothing going on, so with my grandmother passing away, it was a big event. Everybody in the town came to pay their respects to my grandmother. It was an interesting gathering at the Congregational Church in town here.

Seems as uif the line of people was never ending and as people came through and said the same things. “We’re so sorry that your grandmother passed away. She was such a wonderful woman.” I was waiting for somebody to come through and say, “Your grandmother was such an unpleasant woman. She was crabby and mean and I didn’t like her that much.” None of that’s true, but it would have made this funeral a bit more exciting. The reception line here is so long and this is dragging on and on and on.

Hey, I shouldn’t be thinking such negative thoughts. A funeral is already bleak. I need not make it worse by thinking these sorts of real thoughts. A funeral is for us to pay respects. Considering this was my grandmother’s funeral, I definitely need to be more respectful.

Mrs. Tallman came to the line wearing this huge hat that almost looked as if it had a bird stuck on the top of it. When she came through, I could see my mother turn to me to roll her eyes.

When she finally stepped up to my mother, she cleared her throat as if she were ready to deliver out a long speech. “Well, your mother was one of the most interesting women this town has ever seen. She was a phenomenal writer and town historian. Her work covering the infamous Pigman through the years has been so crucial to this town.”

“Pigman?” I asked, laughing and trying to stifle myself. “Mom, you did once say to me that men were pigs.” My mom pivoted and gave me the polite version of asking me nicely to be quiet.

My mom looked around and then looked down at me, “There’s no such thing as Pigman.”

“Oh yes, there is. Our classmates saw it at the high school dance. Actually, many people have claimed they have seen him. How would you know he didn't exist? You don't live here anymore and you haven't for so long," Mrs. Tallman responded, saying a mouthful.

"Well, those are just rumors and a great story. I'm more thankful for what my mother did with keeping this town's history in order." My mom said, trying to sound polite yet firm.

"But it is a part of this town's history," she replied, correcting my mother.

"Well, I guess we will have to agree to disagree," my mom said, trying to end the conversation.

Mrs. Tallman shuffled her feet away and walked out the side door of the church.

"What was that all about?" I asked my mother. As I was slightly dumbfounded that an argument was happening and it wasn't about my grandmother. It was about a Pigman? That even sounded mystifying to me.

"Mrs. Tallman is and always has been a nuisance. She starts rumors and has always been the town's busybody. She is more than annoying. She is trouble." My mom started off the description as nice but Mrs. Tallman wasn't. It was obvious she didn't like her.

"No, Mom, not about that, about this Pigman?" I didn't want to hear about Mrs. Tallman.

"It is just a town fable that's been swirling around for as far back as I can remember." Mom growled with a sense of impatience. "Everyone embellishes the stories and I don't believe any of them, frankly."

"But it still sounds interesting, Mom. Did Grandma ever see Pigman?" I asked, eagerly.

"Yes, she claimed she did." My mom retorted she used to write about interviews with the people that had seen it.

"Have there been many sightings of Pigman?" Inquiring, I hoped that my mom wouldn't get frustrated and end the conversation.

"I've heard them throughout the years. I've heard different versions of them and they're just all lies. People are so bored in this town they just make up stuff to scare people and all it does is give this town more attention than it deserves. I believe *Jack and the Beanstalk* over any Pigman story," she said smiling down on me. "I can't believe Mrs. Tallman would bring up the Pigman at my mother's funeral. Some people are more than annoying." exhaling in one enormous sigh.

"Books?" I asked.

"Oh yes, she wrote a few books through the years, it was her side hobby." It didn't seem to be a big deal to my mom.

"Why didn't you tell me that Grandma was an author?" I asked, as if they had lied to me to all these years.

"Well, Trinity, you knew she was a writer," Mom said, trying to reassure me she didn't intentionally keep it from me.

I was getting a little ticked at my mom. Why would she hold back that information from me? I can understand why she didn't talk about my dad but Grandma we knew, visited her and we talked frequently on the phone.

"Her books are adult romance and I didn't think you were ready to read them. I think you are old enough now, though. Most of what she wrote was for the town newspaper and her infamous Pigman blog and Facebook group." My mom quickly noted, hoping I would just move on.

I was perturbed that I hadn't heard this information until now, especially now that I'm a teenager but I just listened.

"That seems kind of like it's out of place here," I agreed. "Nobody else has mentioned the Pigman at all."

"Yes, because they are not whacked out like Mrs. Tallman," my mother erupted, laughing for the first time on this horrific day that we buried my grandmother.

"Definitely a wackadoodle," I joined in laughing along with my mother.

"I don't know about you but I'm tired of this funeral thing," my mother stated, looking at me. "I am all cried out, I can't take this anymore," my mother announced as she had hit her breaking point.

"I agree, Mom, I've had enough of fake smiling," mimicking the smiling I had been doing all morning.

We both turned and laughed, trying to keep our faces straight as people were surrounding us and were looking sad.

I quickly got out my phone and looked at searching for my grandmother's name. "Mom, I don't see Grandma's books online."

"Oh, they're there. She wrote under a pen name." My mom sputtered quickly in between a sentence with comments made to someone she was talking with. “Her fake name is Urma Applebaum.”

My mom turned around abruptly, before I could respond.

“Cool,” I said to the back of my mom’s head. “Maybe I can pull the fire alarm.” I teased, knowing she would hear me and enjoy the laugh.

My mom‘s belly jiggled as if she tried to stifle her laughter. “Stop! You will get us both in trouble,” she said, trying to scold me in between laughs. “We only have about another hour and then we can go back to Grandma’s house.”

“Yes,” quickly replying to the obvious, “and you know how I am,” I reminded my mother. “We have a lot to do.”

“Trinity, we have a lot to throw away,” my mom stressed in a serious tone, “except for her books and writings, of course. I want you to keep those.” My mom sounded proud now of my grandmother and what she had accomplished. I think this funeral was making her realize my grandmother had made quite an impact in this small town.

First thing I thought of was how grandma’s the opposite of me, a hoarder or pack rat of sorts; though we both liked to write.

I could tell my mother was getting exhausted. She was out of her element being up here in Vermont. I, on the other hand, liked it, even if this town was haunted by a Pigman. I can’t say I’ve ever heard anything like that in Hershey, Pennsylvania.

Knowing my grandmother had no other relatives besides us, I knew we would acquire her house. Gaining her house means gaining her mess.

Her house was absolutely filled with stuff, as I've said before. Now it is all our stuff. I could tell my mother was already processing and had already needed to process the daunting task of driving all the way to my grandmother's house and taking care of all the details. There were so many details to be taken care of and I knew her house was one of them. I knew we would probably be there the whole summer. My talents and gifts will be used full time, 24/7. I guess it's a good thing I am who I am. The task ahead was overwhelming to my mother but the two of us quickly formed a team.

Chapter 3
The Typewriter Type

They have always known me as a neat freak, that's for sure.

So When Mom told me the news of Grandma passing, it was sad, and it hurt me. Then when she looked at me and announced it was our job to clean out her house, it was a bittersweet feeling.

I mean, come on, going through someone else's house is a bit freaky. You're going through someone's stuff, and you owned none of it. None of it is yours. You are a visitor and now it is your house. My mom and I will not live here but we need to get rid of all this stuff so we can sell the house.

On the ride up from Pennsylvania, mom declared she might even consider keeping this house so we can come here each summer. I'm not sure I like that idea either. This is a cool town and all but I don't really have any friends here. Back home my friends would be all gone each summer anyway doing their own things. Some of my friends go to different states to stay in their parents' summer homes. Other friends of mine go to sports camps. I'm not interested in that either. So maybe coming here for the summer is a cool idea.

So June came and Mom and I returned here to Vermont to work on the house. The air was musty and it smelled like newspapers everywhere. My grandmother was definitely a hoarder. Though she would never admit it and she really didn't have to clean for anybody but herself. We never went there for family holidays or anything. She would come to our house once a year for about a week or so and, as Mom said; she would wear out her welcome. So we never really came here often but we had our times here, which was cool. It might be nice for us to stay here all summer and really get to know people. I think it would be respectful to my grandmother.

I can FaceTime all my friends anyway, so it's not like we would hang out at home with them right now.

The town librarian came and visited us and told us we needed to create a pile for her so she could take whatever were historical documents of the town. We would put them all in one pile and she would come and get them so she could store them at the town library. I was all for that as was my mom. It would make the house so much less cluttered.

Overall, the house wasn't the worst thing I'd ever seen. I watched that show before where they go into hoarder's houses and try to fix them; meaning—try to make the people realize they had an issue. I would say because my grandmother lived alone she didn't really need to worry about anything. It wasn't as if she had anybody living in the bedrooms except her. She didn't have anybody else for whom to cook. I almost envied her, as there really was nobody to impress.

My mom isn't really a neat freak. She really isn't as clean as me; but I know being here at Grandma's house, she'll want to throw a bunch of things away. I know she has some memories that make her sad and should probably keep those things; however, overall I know she will want to just keep feeding the dumpster that's in the driveway. My mom rented it so we could just throw things in there and they would come at the end of the week to empty it. The dumpster is huge and I can just barely throw things over the side of it. I know we will fill it, probably a few times.

Anyway, I think it will be exciting to see what treasures we find. I know that I'm keeping a box or two just for myself. I cannot wait to find cool things.

My grandmother was the town historian, so of anything that had to do with history or artifacts she was in charge. There is a town museum down the road where all the big things are stored. This town is somewhat interesting because there's a museum, but it isn't open much. I'm sure there aren't many people who come to look at old things. I know there's like a covered wagon in there and some things from hundreds of years ago. The town museum is where the one-room schoolhouse used to be. So, my grandmother has a ton of things for that as well as the original schoolhouse. It is set up to look just like it did back in the 1800s.

There are literally stacks and stacks of newspapers everywhere. So we will donate these to the town library. They go back all the way to when my grandmother started writing articles for the town newspaper. Also, it looks as if my grandmother printed out every blog and Facebook article she ever wrote. She did a ton of writing online too, which always made her a cool grandma to me. She was always similar to my posts, even the ones my mom made me take down later on because she thought they were inappropriate. I like to talk my mind and I like to write what I'm thinking about things. I have my opinions about life and politics and, sometimes, my mom said they were embarrassing. So, I took them down. I didn't argue with her but I could see why she would find them maybe too controversial. My mom's a really low key person. My grandmother wasn't.

If there was a town issue or problem, my grandmother was right in the middle of it. She was always good about looking at all sides of an argument. She wouldn't just take one side and run with it, she gave both and actually several points of view.

I always thought it was interesting she would look at all the political candidates for a race not just the two sides. She thought one should look at all types of thinking. Maybe that's why she and my mother didn't get along. My mom is wonderful and

I'm not complaining about her, however, if she disagrees with you, she will let you know quickly and sometimes loudly.

So I'm really not sure what to do. *Should I keep all the things my grandmother has written or just throw them away and know that I can access them anytime I want at the town library?* I'm not sure what I want to do as I don't want to take a bunch of stuff home to clutter my room. My room is exactly how I want it, and I don't want to collect more things.

I like to write, the same as my grandmother. I find writing to be relaxing and a way to have somebody to whom to talk. I know when I write there will not be any arguments or yelling. I know when I am alone and either typing or writing on paper, my thoughts are secure. My thoughts are safe. I know I'm not offending anybody because I'm just trying to organize my thoughts about something.

It's this way, I see a presidential debate on the TV and it's just people yelling at each other. It is two people passionate about opposing viewpoints. For instance, one person likes the regular Oreos and I like the double stuff. Or they like the vanilla Oreos and I like the chocolate ones. Just because we believe something different, we get so passionate about it now our voices are raised. To me, writing is a way to get it out on paper and for me to look at it and for it to be calm. When somebody states their opinion calmly more people are apt to listen. When there is shouting, all you think about is the yelling and not what they are trying to say.

I would listen to my mom and grandmother on the phone and it would start quietly. They would start talking about things then it would turn to maybe what was going on in the news or maybe a viewpoint about money or maybe it was my mother telling my grandmother she wasn't taking good enough care of herself. She would get sick if she didn't eat a certain way or eat healthy. She would often ask my grandmother if she was exercising. My grandmother would respond, "Well, I'm a writer and historian, I can't really do that on an exercise bike or while I'm walking." My mother would get concerned and start talking to her as if she were her child. My grandmother would not tolerate that. It would soon become a heated argument where my mom would hang up on her and not talk to her for maybe two months.

My mom already told me up front, "You can only take home two typewriters from Grandma's house." What can I say? I enjoy using typewriters. I think they're classy. It's a cool way to type out writing and I think it makes you go a little slower than on the computer. Word processing on the computer you can make mistakes and always go back and fix them, whereas when you're typing on a typewriter you have to be more calm and collected. I think that's a cool idea. Sometimes I like to type on the computer because I can save it and go back and change it. Sometimes though, I choose to type my final draft for school, if I'm working on a project, on a typewriter because I go slower and think before I type. If you make a mistake, you can use Whiteout and type over it. That's kind of cool to me. My mother told me she will donate the real old ones to the town museum. I don't want those, anyway. Those will just clutter up my room and you know how I am. I want to take home two of her newer typewriters. Right until her death, she used a typewriter on a lot of her newspaper stories. In fact, the typewriter looks like that newsprint. It's that courier font that I like to use. It's that old school typing to me that makes writing sometimes even more interesting. So I really have to look through each one and see which one would be the best one to take home. Then take a second one as a backup; so I will have to do my research online to see which one has ribbon available. Typewriter ribbon is what the keys hit to put the ink on the paper. It's kind of an interesting setup because we're used to printers printing on paper. With a typewriter, you are kind of in charge of every letter that goes on the paper. So you strike the key with your finger and it brings that letter up to hit the ribbon onto the paper. I don't know if I'm explaining it well, but you could YouTube a video to look at it. Anyway, I need to see what ribbon is easily available that I can order on Amazon and have plenty of it when I run out.

So with all that being said, I will approach cleaning my grandmother's house probably a little differently from the way my mother will. I think if it was up to my mother she would take a bulldozer and just bulldoze the house or find a bulldozer to bulldoze through the house. Or if there was a way just to collect everything in there and throw it in a dumpster, she would do it without even looking through things. If there was a way to rig a vacuum hose that went directly to the dumpster outside, I'm sure my mom would have bought or rented it by now. I don't think cleaning my grandmother's house will take only a few days. I think we will be here the whole summer and that's OK with me. I know it will be impossible to look through everything in this house but there are definitely things I want to keep.

Hey, I like to write what's wrong with that. So did my grandmother. So I guess through this process I will have to stick up for her, even though she's not here anymore.

Chapter 4

A Stroll Down Devil's Washbowl Lane

I knew the next morning my mother would be up early getting a game plan. We only had about six days to be here to work before we had to be back to Hershey. My mother didn't like taking days off from work because she didn't get a ton of vacation time each year. This was a little different as it was the death of her own mother, so they gave her a different type of time off.

Before I could even wake up and know what I was doing, my mother showed up with my favorite donuts and two coffees.

"Mom, I didn't think you wanted me to drink coffee. You said it would stunt my growth. We know that's not true. I'm already taller than you," telling Mom the truth. I had just passed her in height.

My mom laughed aloud. She seemed at ease and definitely ready to seize the day.

"That is a good point, Trin. You are now taller than your mother. I just want to get started so we can get as much done as we can in these next few days. I think it's best if we just stayed focused on this so we can try to get it all done and get out of here." My mom gulped, sounding as if we were in some prison just waiting to be released.

"I agree, Mom, and I am glad you made it through yesterday. I could tell it wasn't easy on you." Speaking these words to my mom made me sound more like we were friends. That was OK with me. My mom looked down at the floor and then looked at me and gave a slight nod.

"It was not a good day and I think it's good to have all this behind us. I never really took time to think about the truth I would bury my mother. Sometimes I think I made myself so busy with work so I wouldn't have the time to think about death. I figured death would do the thinking for me but it is me who has to process the death of grandma." She was speaking as if she were confessing something to me. Something I already could see as she was always working. I didn't respond to her as she was getting it all out. The pause in the conversation was my mom getting the time she needed to carry out her thoughts. I didn't want to interrupt them. This was good. Groundbreaking. The last thing I wanted to do was get her off this healthy path of thinking, reflecting and communicating it.

I waited.

"Anyway, I am glad to be here with you and tackling this project together," she spoke to break the silence.

"I'm ready to go if you are, Mom." I was actually motivated to help so we could get back to civilization. It was quiet here, that's for sure. I could definitely hear myself think. Plus, I wanted to pick through the typewriters and find the two I would be allowed to take home. If I found a third one I really would want that might make its way into the trunk somewhere in our car.

"What is this big box on the dining room table for, Mom?" I asked, because I hadn't seen it there before.

"Oh, that's what I want to explain to you so what we will be doing is the books and pieces that are marked, 'Historical Society,' are going to go in this box and the town librarian who will be picking them up and bringing them to the library. The Town Board met and decided from now on to have the town's Historical Society located right at the library.

"Sounds official, so that must be a good idea," I responded, not knowing what it was all about. "That is good that we are not throwing away the town's history."

"Exactly, Trinity, and she will be over to pick them up periodically throughout the week while we're here so we can just keep filling the box," she instructed me, as if I was the one throwing everything away. I don't think so.

"I like being organized but I am not a minimalist." I announced, declaring the facts because my mom is prone to throwing things away.

"Let's eat our bagels first, I am too hungry to start this project yet," Mom insisted, with a cool sense of reality. Eating is always the key to starting anything.

"You got a bagel? Oh no, I was hoping for donuts." I whined, disappointed as I had assumed what was in the bag.

"Trinity. I got both." She joked with a huge smile, pulling them both out of the bag.

It was somewhat surreal with Mom and I actually getting along to a point where we could work on a project together. We had definitely different points of view of cleanliness, that's for sure.

"Mom, I think somebody's pulling in the driveway," speaking over her as I was alarmed that someone would be here so early in the morning.

Looking out the front bay window, "that is Janet, she is here already so let's put these two stacks of books in there so she can take them and get them out of our way."

"Good morning, Janet, come on in," my mother greeted her at the door and you could tell they had known each other for a long time.

Turning to introduce me to her, "Trinity, this is Janet, she is the town librarian and will now be the part-time town historian. She's taking over for your grandmother. Janet and I went to school together here in Northfield."

"Sweet," I nodded, as I shook her hand.

"And this is her daughter Katrina," Mom informed me as Katrina gave me an awkward look, like I don't really want to be here but I have to and a weak wave.

I knew I needed to break this awkward silence, "Hey, it looks like you got dragged into this mess with me too." I jested as my mom and her mom went off into the dining room where the books and boxes were located.

"Sure did. I got roped into helping my mom bring all these books to the library so I am not too thrilled about it," Katrina related, making it obvious this wasn't high among her priorities.

"No, me either, as I don't really want to be here working on this overwhelming mess, as I'd rather be home enjoying my spring break. I like to be organized but this house is just going to get sold, so I don't really care as much," I admitted, eking out the truth, just a little. I could tell she was looking at me as if she were really not happy to be hauling books around on her break.

My mom appeared behind us. It was almost as if she either sensed we weren't thrilled with things or she and Janet needed to discuss something with us, far away. "Why don't you go for a walk while Janet and I catch up on things." She suggested to us, almost telling us politely to go.

"Great idea, Mom," I agreed readily, with a respectful smile and wink to my mom.

"Can you show me around this town? I think I might need another donut." Speaking the truth and Katrina instantly giggled. Either what I said was funny to her or she was thinking the same thing about a donut.

"I know what you're saying and I agree, it is a boring town. That's why most of life is online and not here. The only interesting thing in this time was actually your grandmother and my grandmother." She conversed about it like it was common knowledge.

I stopped mid-step on the sidewalk and turned towards Katrina, "I am not following what you are saying. This town is anything but exciting," realizing that I might be rude. "Oh yeah, who's your grandmother?"

"You met her yesterday at the funeral. Her name is Alicia Tallman." She spoke with confidence, as if she saw me meet her.

Hitting me as I blocked out most of the funeral as they aren't really my thing, "Oh my gosh, I completely forgot about her. She was the only one that said something different and interesting in that whole long line of people saying the same thing repeatedly. Sorry about your grandmother. Sorry about your grandmother." I was rambling, and I needed to stop.

"My gram is out there for sure and that makes her so cool. I think coolness skipped our mothers' generation," Katrina said then erupted into laughter.

I shrieked and buckled over in laughter, "you nailed it, Katrina. My mom is as exciting as watching paint dry sometimes. You know, she ticked my mom off at the funeral because she mentioned a thing about a Pigman and how my grandmother used to write about the Pigman sightings in this town," I related then laughed aloud and thought about that for a split second. I was thinking all the thousands of times I had texted someone "LOL" but was not laughing aloud or really even laughing. This time it was legit.

"Exactly, that's why I'm saying they were the only two interesting people in this town. Everything else is all about slow internet, town budgets and basically all that nothing there is to do here." Katrina spoke sounding depressed.

"I agree with you but I'm starting to kind of like it here. It's different from Hershey, Pennsylvania. It is just different, not worse. Sometimes it is too noisy in Hershey." I empathize trying to make Katrina see the good in the town she lived in. There was nothing wrong with Northfield, Vermont. It was pleasant and quiet.

"How cool you are from Hershey, Pennsylvania? She replied instantly as if a little lightbulb went on in her brain snapping her out of her disdain for her town. We visited there a few years ago and I absolutely loved it. I can't wait to go back there again."

"Some people call it the land of chocolate or where chocolate was born. That's cool and all but I like Ghirardelli chocolate better than Hershey's." I confessed in an actual proud way. Speaking my mind made me feel better about myself.

Katrina looked at me in a slightly worried way, almost as if she couldn't believe what I was saying. I reassured her it was just a difference of preference.

I broke the silence with, "Katrina, now you have an extra reason to go visit Hershey."

"I do?" Katrina questioned, looking confused.

"Yeah, me," I blurted, as if she and I had been friends for years instead of my having just met her.

Katrina sighed, "You know you are right. Summer is coming soon and I am already dreading being stuck in this place."

"Let's talk Pigman, Katrina; I need you to tell what this is really all about." I could almost tell Katrina probably believed in it, so I wanted to make sure I didn't sound skeptical.

"OK, well then let's not walk downtown. Let's walk up out of town a little." She suggested as we crossed the road and started walking off the sidewalk and onto a road.

"Why would we do that?" I inquired, as I wasn't making the connection of why changing where we walked determined her telling me about the Pigman.

"So I will take you up the road a little way to Devil's Washbowl," Katrina instructed and informed as if she were a tour guide.

"What is that?" I wondered if she was actually just trying to freak me out and scare me, and it would be nothing. She didn't seem to be that type but I wasn't sure.

"This is the road where most of the sightings took place," she pointed out, as if she had said it many times and it was just part of the lore of this sleepy town.

I was definitely interested, even if it would turn out to be nothing. It was better than just sitting around a pile of books. “Absolutely, let’s go now.”

“So, I should probably start with the beginning of this story that took place a long time ago.” Katrina noted. It was beginning to sound as a “once upon a time,” folktale.

“Oh, so this is a once upon a time a long time ago type of fable?” I quoted with a slightly cynical tone in my voice. I was just testing her and letting her know I wasn’t a gullible child.

“Now, I am sure the first Pigman sighting was when our grandmothers were at their senior prom down at the high school gymnasium,” she recollected but I think she had probably heard so many stories through the years.

“Oh, really? That’s odd. A Pigman showed up at the prom?” I didn’t know much about the Pigman in that my mother never really talked about it and the mention of it had bothered my mother at the funeral.

“Yep, that’s where the entire story started. There was a kid that went missing a few years before the first sighting and they always thought he had changed or acted like a pig trying to survive in the woods by himself.” She speculated with some uncertainty about exactly how the Pigman came about.

“Katrina, by looking around here and actually this entire town, there is nothing but woods around here. I can see where that would happen. Just looking at the forest up there, it seems as if it goes on for miles and miles,” I marveled as I turned and looked at the panoramic view of the high hills.

"That's exactly where people have seen him." She explained to me. "In fact, I don't even know if your mom knows this but our grandmothers used to do Pigman tours for people's right until your grandmother passed away."

"Are you kidding me? Whoa, that is so cool. I have always begged my mother to let me go on a ghost tour near to where we live. You get to stay the night in an old abandoned asylum." I related to her as if we were on the same page of how this was interesting.

Well, think about it, Trinity, what else are you going to do in this town? People came from all over the country and world in hope of catching a glimpse of the infamous Pigman." She said, making it sound even more real and even more important than I thought it was.

"Good point, Katrina," I agreed with her.

People from afar would come here and stay here and take their tour. They would also want to learn more about the Pigman sightings because there were so many and there was a lot of proof. It wasn't just some grainy pictures or videos that you couldn't tell exactly what it was," sounding as if she were trying to sell me the whole concept of the Pigman. I was definitely starting to see this was an area of passion for her.

Asking for more clarification, I said, "So they would start the tour up here in Devil's Washbowl and they would see the Pigman?"

"I don't have that answer but I've been on the tour before because my parents were out of town and I had to stay with my grandmother," Katrina replied.

"Do you believe in all this too?" I asked Katrina point blank because I was curious.

"I don't know for sure. Sometimes I do and other times I doubt it all but I can just tell you what I've heard." She speculated diplomatically, sounding as if she didn't want to offend anyone.

I am wondering, especially if there are many sightings," I responded, wanting Katrina to share more. I wasn't sure what to believe but I wanted to hear more.

"They start the tour right at the school. Right down at the old high school in the back where the parking lot is located. They start there because that's where some of their friends saw the Pigman for the first time at the senior prom that year. The dance was going on just like any other normal prom-like setting and then it got hot in the gymnasium so they opened the doors and some people were too hot so they just went outside to hang out in the cool early June evening air. There was a small group of them outside then they came running in, all freaked out. They said they had been standing there talking and they heard this growling and loud chomping sound right beyond the parking lot in the bushes. Apparently what happened was they saw a creature jump out of the woods. It had white hair and a kind of pink skin like a pig and the head was almost identical to that of a pig with a nose and everything. Some teens thought they were just pulling a prank but they could see the creature was devouring an animal, something that he had evidently taken from a local farm."

"Why didn't they call the police?" I interjected, wondering about it as it was sounding out of control.

"They did," Katrina replied and continued her story. "So the police arrived and they investigated it. They could see where the grass was all trampled down and into the woods. They found animal carcasses and bones. They did not see any of the creatures they had claimed they had seen. So they filled out a police report and they each identified the creature almost identically." Katrina repeated, and I was certain she had heard this story many times. She seemed to know it well.

"OK, so why were their sightings of all places up here on this road?" I asked, trying to see how this made sense.

"Well, Trinity, there was a young boy that had gone missing a few years earlier. They believed he got lost in the woods."

I was getting concerned, especially if there was a missing child, "He went missing, how young was he?"

"Allegedly, he was about sixteen and had gone missing a couple years prior to the sighting. So they originally thought it was him. In fact, he lived up here on a farm right on Devil's Washbowl."

That would have made him approximately the same age of our grandmothers, I thought but didn't share it. "OK, so I'm not connecting how these two are alike because this is a sighting of a man that was a pig."

"Well, apparently after they had seen the creature at the dance or the school prom, they reopened the investigation to look for him. So they scoured the woods beyond the farm up here on the hill. So right up past here is a river with waterfalls and there's a bunch of caves. So they found up in the caves that these different caves were filled with animal bones and different sets of human clothes that look like they've been worn by the same person. He also found that there had been small campfires in each location." She listed sharing a lot of information to me and I was getting places and sightings confused. This was a lot of information to process on what was supposed to be a leisurely walk to get away from cleaning an entire house.

"That could be just kids playing around or could be campers or something that just makes little sense. Who is this kid that went missing?" I wondered if this was just a typical legend.

"According to the locals, they call him Sam Harris." Katrina said.

"That's kind of freaky and creepy to think someone got lost in the woods and then reappeared as a Pigman," I responded, almost making my own assumptions without really examining all the facts

"So there's a farmer right up here on the left who was asleep one night and heard something going through the trash, and he thought it was a bear. When he turned on the yard-light out back and saw a man rummaging through his garbage he made eye contact with him. It was the same description as the high schoolers gave of who they saw that night at the prom." as Katrina pointed up at an old farmhouse that looked to be in awful shape.

It was making the hair on the back of my neck stand up. I was getting slightly creeped out.

"It's definitely freaky but that's not even half of it." Katrina continued. "The Farmer called the police and they put bloodhounds on his scent and it led back to a cave that was empty. It was the one cave where they had found the clothes, the old campfire and the animal bones."

"Wow, this is a lot more in-depth than I thought," I said, concerned that some human was living in a cave up here.

"As time went on, the Pigman seemed to get more violent and the sightings were more dangerous. Of course, that made everybody in this town terrified of this area. In fact, they could never even sell a home up this road for years and years because of it," she informed me, which was making sense to me now. The houses up here looked old and not kept up well.

"This is changing from a few sightings to many actual stories," I stated, interested in learning more about this.

"What happened was a lot of teenagers would come and camp out here so they could try to get a glimpse of the Pigman, and sometimes it didn't work out well. I know some of them were making false claims and some stories were proven to be lies. There were a few, though that are interesting storie,." Katrina affirmed.

"It seems like when there's a sighting of something then numerous copycats or fake types of stories surface." Katrina reported to me as if this was a news story. "I heard one night some teens were up there camping and one of them got attacked and got scratches on his chest and arm from the Pigman and the other campers could hear it squealing. They brought the police in to investigate, and they had photos of the person who was hurt. In fact, he still lives in this town and he is quite bothered by it and doesn't want to talk about it. If you are interested, there is an interview of him and it is actually on YouTube if you ever want to watch it. He allowed his recollection of that evening to be videoed but he will not answer anyone's questions in person. I guess he's still pretty messed up from the incident that happened years ago."

"I would be too. That sounds crazy disgusting," I said, even more interested in this Pigman thing even though someone was hurt. That wasn't cool but it made me think *this is scary real.*

"There is so much to tell you," Katrina said, "a few years later, a group of teenagers wanted to catch him on video. So they actually slept in one of the caves up there. They were there for a few days and saw nothing but about three days in there were six of them sleeping. The Pigman came in and struck one of them on the head with a rock then picked the man up to move him. The other five woke up and startled him and he started running. So a few of them drove into town and alerted the police. They all came back with weapons to hunt down the Pigman. The police arrived with their canine units and the state police were called in to look for the Pigman. A few days later I guess they retrieved some articles of clothing that were found by a search dog, but that was about it."

"That is wild. What was going on around here, Katrina? Why would our grandmothers want to do tours if something so sinister was lurking here in the woods?" Just asking that made me not really want to be hanging around here. Not that I easily get freaked out but the sightings seem to be anything but entertaining.

"So that's why my grandmother and your grandmother would have to spend hours sifting through the different stories to see which ones were real and which ones were just fake. The stories all sounded the same. I'm not sure what to believe right now. Since I was little I've heard hundreds of different stories. It proved some to be true and others were not. Our grandmothers have really worked hard to find the legitimate claims and to write about them." Katrina said, making things sound less scary to me.

"Yeah, I can see why they were both busy, if, for years, it's been chaotic here. It is easy to make a quiet town turn loud. Plus, I am sure there were many false rumors going around and they wanted people to be informed with accurate information," I added.

"It comes and goes. Sometimes there've been sightings then you don't hear anything for a year or two. Then there'll be resurgence. News crews come here trying to get the story so they can write about it. That's where your grandmother handled most of the public relations when it came to the Pigman. She was well-known with many people for all the research she did. That's why she will definitely be missed in this town," Katrina humbly acknowledged.

"My grandmother's death was such a surprise to us. I don't think it has really sunk with my mother yet. She hasn't accepted the reality she'll never see her mother again. It's been hard on us but my mother really never got along with my grandmother anyway, so it makes it more awkward being here. This is where my mother grew up yet she really hasn't been back here since she was eighteen for more than two or three days at a time and that was because we were here to visit her mother," she spilled the truth.

"And another thing was, our grandmothers would get ridiculed by certain people who didn't believe in any of this. There are many locals who said it is too hard to believe. Even though Pigman was seen by many, they just don't seem to think it was true. So, if anyone mentions the Pigman, it can be a sore subject," muttered Katrina, with a face of slight disgust. Almost as if she were siding with her grandmother.

"That's pretty sad they would put them down, especially when locals have seen it and gotten hurt from the Pigman himself," I replied, sympathetically.

"Some of them were petrified for years because of the Pigman. Some still definitely are," Katrina clarified as she stared up the field into the hills.

"Katrina, it sounds like the sightings have never really gone away have they?" I asked.

"No, they haven't. In fact, you hear a lot of sightings from hunters each fall during deer season. We have a lot of hunters that come up in this area and some are from out of state and they have seen what appears to be a man that resembles a pig running around in the woods," said Katrina, as I stood and walked back down the road.

"If so many people are seeing it, it's got to be true," I said, thinking aloud, trying to reason out all this information that I was hearing for the first time.

"Trinity, just from talking to you about it, I believe it's true because for so many years our entire life has been all about it because that's all my grandmother would ever talk about and still do to this day," she added.

I turned and faced Katrina, "I would love to pick your grandmother's brain. I'm sure she's got a lot of cool stories."

"She definitely does. She would love to talk to you about it and that would be good for you because then you could hear more about all your grandmother did for this town."

"I don't think I'm going to get good stories for my mother about my grandmother as they used to argue quite a bit," I said.

"Let's head back to your grandmother's house and then we can hang out later in the week," Katrina suggested, "my mom just texted, and she is ready to leave."

"That's right, I totally forgot we are cleaning out my grandmother's entire house. This will be such a pain," I protested.

"I'll give you a chance to look through all her cool stuff. I know you're giving stuff to my mother for the library and it'll give me an excuse to come back later in the week to talk to you." Katrina added thoughtfully.

“Please do as I know I will go crazy cleaning 24/7.”

Katrina actually laughed aloud again, “I can totally understand that, Trinity.”

Chapter 5

Room in the Writing Room

"Well, it is past noon on our first cleaning day here Trin, we better get moving as I am missing Hershey." My mom informed me.

"No doubt, Mom, me too and I know my friends are missing me. I am getting so many 'I miss you' snapchats. I informed her, showing her the screenshots I had taken.

"I just want to be back home. This house has always sort of given me the creeps." Mom complained, looking at an old picture which must have been my triple great grandfather.

"Mom, you grew up here," thinking I was reminding her of the obvious.

"No, I didn't," she quickly responded to me. "We moved here when I was about your age. So, I never got a feel of home. It was where I really grew up. The first thirteen years of my life we lived down on the other end of town in a big farmhouse."

"Why have you never told me or showed me that all the times we have been here?" I asked as if I were missing some obvious information about my mom that she should have told me years ago.

"Because I am still bugged by it," Mom chirped back and sounded a little snippy.

"Mom, let it go. We live in an apartment," I reminded her. "So, I would be happy to have a house this size."

"This big? My mom said with a slight edge. "What would you and I do with all this room?"

"Fill it, Mom, with typewriters, friends and happiness." I improvised, making it up as I went. "Then you could just throw it all away when I was away at camp or something."

"Trin, you are in so much trouble." My mom muttered, rolling her eyes at me. "I guess you are right, there is no reason not to like this house."

"It smells like newspapers and potpourri," I kindly reminded her.

"Well, at the old house, your grandmother used to have cows and chickens, and let me tell you, they didn't always smell good." She instructed as if I didn't know those smells.

"That is disgusting, Mom," I gagged, pinching my nose.

"OK, OK let's get cleaning," Mom chuckled, tossing junk into the dumpster.

"The first thing I am going to do is to look for Grandma's typewriters."

"They are all downstairs in her 'writing room', as she called it," Mom said, sounding slightly uninterested. The last thing she wants to talk about is typewriters.

"Oh yeah, that's right Mom," I said quickly to just move on so I could get digging. I was excited and energetic but still sad. I walked swiftly down the stairs.

"I will start up here with this huge mound on the dining room table," she said but it was fading as I was down under her on the bottom level of the house but walked back up as I knew she was still talking.

Mom knew the messy table had been driving me nuts since I got here. I cannot stand looking at messes but my feelings of sympathy toward my mother stifled any negative thinking. There is a time to just be silent.

"I know this would never be allowed at home as you would clean it until it was done," Mom said lovingly, knowing I was just trying to help. Mom has always been patient with my 'need to clean'.

Grandma's writing room wasn't as messy as the rest of her house but I knew the good stuff was in there; more specifically, her typewriter collection.

"OK, Mom, I will start down there and start a pile to throw away. I promise." Assuring my mom, I had good intentions and wanted to be back in Pennsylvania.

"Thanks Trin, I couldn't do this without you. It is too depressing. It is a nice trip down memory lane; however some memories aren't too pleasant."

Mom confided, peering down the stairs, getting my eye contact.

"Mom, you two are different. Different doesn't mean it is bad. It is just two different ways to see things. One isn't wrong," I was assuming what she was thinking based on our conversation over breakfast the day before.

"Yes, Dr. Trinity," my mother acknowledged, knowing I was right and knowing I was much like my grandmother. "You are right and I am thankful for who you are, Trin."

"That's Dr. Trinity Porter to you mom," I said laughing and knowing it was a good time to break off the conversation and get busy. "I will send you a bill for my services," making my voice louder as I started walking back downstairs. My grandmother's house is a raised ranch style home to the downstairs eye level to the ground. Her office and writing table were up against the window so she could see the beautiful front yard and gardens. I am sure she positioned it that way to see if someone was pulling into the garage.

Doing a scan of the entire room, I could see about eight different typewriters. Four or five of them look like they hadn't been touched in years and were just collecting dust. There was however one typewriter that had a cover on it over to the side. It appeared she only used it on special occasions. Taking the cover off, I could see that I was right. It was a high-end model that really was one of the best there is. In fact, I only saw them in magazines. I didn't even know my grandmother had one of these.

I put that by the door immediately as I know my grandmother would want me to have this one. She knows I'll put it to good use. I jumped online quickly and saw that ribbon for this typewriter was inexpensive and easy to get.

Looking down next to her printer was an entire stack of Pigman tour brochures. That did kind of make me laugh a little because it sounds like a crazy idea.

What excited me was there was a small pile of books that looked like my grandmother was about to mail out before she passed away. Opening them up to the title page, I could see that she had autographed them with her pen name. Urma Applebaum, in big, bold, cursive letters. *Should I should mail these? They paid for them. I'll set them aside to bring upstairs.*

My grandmother had always been interesting to me. She was organized, sort of. In her own way, I am sure she knew where everything was. She developed her own filing system of piles. She had one pile for the local newspaper. She had another pile for her online blog. She had a pile of newspapers that were local and statewide. She also had a pile of stuff for ideas in terms of her next, but appeared I'm so confused. It seems it was such a big part of her life and there's literally nothing here in her writing room that shows she did any real research on the Pigman. I figured from what Katrina had told me earlier today this room would be filled with stuff surrounding all the sightings.

My eyes moved around the room at everything. Typewriters and piles. Interestingly enough, though, I didn't see really any piles in her office that had to do with a Pigman, except for the few brochures that I found. Anyway, I'm so glad I can see through all that my grandmother accomplished in her life, it's very interesting.

Well, I have one typewriter chosen and I think I have my eye on a second one.

This one is a classic and I might use this one from time to time. I'm not sure though.

I'm feeling a little sad my grandmother's gone now and I'm looking through her stuff. I kind of feel as if I'm almost spying on her. I wouldn't want that if I were alive. I think it's kind of creepy once we're gone, our stuff is just there for anybody to take, really. I know I wouldn't want anybody snooping through my room. I get grumpy when even my mom comes in just to borrow a pen or something.

I definitely think I want this other typewriter.

It definitely is a little dusty though, but looking at all the other typewriters it's one of the more current ones.

Lifting it up, I noticed underneath it there was a key. It wasn't a creepy skeleton key or anything; it was just a normal, modern key. *Now this will bother me. What in the world does this key go to?* As you know a thousand different things were zipping through my brain. *Does grandma have a hidden safe somewhere? Or one of those storage lockers?* I put the key in my pocket for safekeeping.

Beyond the typewriter was a State of Vermont flag. It was huge, as big as one you would see flying outside on a flagpole. Interesting, in fact, I find all flags interesting. If you look at all the flags throughout the world, they're all so different. It will be a little reminder in Pennsylvania that I was in Vermont. This will look perfect hanging in my room.

When I went to grab it, the flag was thumb tacked to the wall. Behind the thumbtacks was a door that went under the stairs. It was locked. It appeared to have a deadbolt lock. Immediately, I took the key out of my pocket. It was as if I knew it would fit but had no clue if it would.

It slid right in perfectly. It turned, making a real quiet clicking sound.

I was glad my mother wasn't down here.

Opening the door, a slight breeze of colder air rolled out and up to my nose. It smelled different, almost as iuf it hadn't been visited in quite some time. The door, as I could first see it, went into a small room. In fact, it went back out of the room to look around to see how big this room would have been. They built it at the bottom of the stairs on this raised ranch. It was a big enough space. Inside were several boxes and even some clothing, it looked like.

It didn't have the feel of a storage space, or an attic or crawl space. That, to me, makes it slightly alarming. "I think I watch too many scary movies." I concluded aloud, smiling.

Next to the boxes was an army cot. Like a tiny little bed that would fold out that could fit one person, one adult, probably. It also had a pillow on it and it seemed to have a wooden frame, The bed itself felt to be canvas.

Why would my grandmother have a door that was hidden by a flag? Why would she have to hide and lock a room that was filled with boxes of what appeared to be junk? Plus, there is a cot as if somebody could live in here. There are no windows but the light bulbs were LED so I know the room wasn't that old. There wasn't an old hanging light bulb from the ceiling as those in some horror movie. It was definitely modern. In fact, you could say it was even more modern than the rest of the house, in terms of how it was lit.

I immediately thought of Katrina but I didn't want to call her. *I don't know her well enough yet and I'm definitely not going to tell my mother about this room.* So I turned the lights off and locked the door and put the flag back in place.

My mother was getting frustrated upstairs. I could hear her moving things aggressively and items hitting the floor above me. I knew she would be downstairs in about thirty seconds. I didn't want her to see what I had discovered. Not yet, at least. *"It is just another reason your grandmother annoyed me," I can hear my mother speaking those words if she were here with me looking in this odd little room. I don't want to hear her opinion. Plus, maybe this is where she hid her best typewriters. Or maybe cash? If so, I can go to Starbucks every day and fill my cart at Target. What am I doing? I am not a greedy person or a thief but I do like Iced Macchiato.*

I knew my mother was planning to visit the attorney tomorrow morning, so I knew I had time tomorrow morning to pick through this room. How cool! Plus, this makes the cleaning more interesting.

I must investigate this room more but it will have to be tomorrow.

Chapter 6
The Finer Diner

"I need to go to the attorneys at 10:30 and sign some papers. Let's go to the diner and eat breakfast before we go." My mom said, waking me up with her list of to-dos. There was no "good mornings".

"Mom. Why can't you wake me up by saying, good morning, my special, wonderful daughter?" I retorted facetiously, with my eye still stuck shut. My allergies were bothering me a little way up here in the Green Mountains.

"Oh," she paused and looked down at my tired eyes with her high energy. "Good morning, the wonderful and extra special Trinity."

"Why are you a morning person, Mom?" I asked, half wondering why she needed to wake me up.

"That sounds like a good idea but I want to come back here and work on things while you are at the attorneys. That sounds like a long boring meeting." I added being woken up by the possibility of being stuck at some worthless meeting.

"I think you're right, it will probably take a while. I have to look through all the deeds and read through her will." Mom clarified, looking at a list she was holding in her hand. "But let's go get breakfast first."

That woke me up and I was dressed and out in the car within five minutes. I guess I am a little different; I don't need an entire hour to get ready in the morning, especially if breakfast is involved. The diner was less than a mile from grandma's house. I was thankful for that.

"It's so dreamlike to be back in this diner. I've never really been back here since I was probably seventeen. My friends and I used to come here a lot to eat and just try to figure out how we would be famous in life," My mom said, looking around, examining everything on the wall.

"Mom, we do the same things," I said, laughing aloud.

"That is true, Trinity, and I know you can be anything you want to be as you really are an interesting person. I am very thankful to be here with you and working on this project of cleaning Grandma's house out together," my mom was saying quite a lot to me in one breath.

"It's not on the top of my list in terms of things that are cool but it is interesting to see all of Grandma's typewriters and to know she made her living as a writer. I will do all of my homework on them."

"Yes, she certainly did. She didn't really have a lot of money or even any retirement saved and she had to work right up until she passed away; but I guess there's not a bad thing," my mom declared, with some pity in her voice toward my grandmother.

"Well, Mom, I wouldn't say too much, you are always working," I retorted nicely, as it was true.

"Yes, because I have to." My mom inserted in a short, cutting way.

"Yes, Mom, you have to and so did Grandma and I will have to as well. That's kind of how life goes. I think it is neat Grandma made money in so many ways in this small town." I encouraged, sticking up for both my grandma and my mother.

"Oh, I know, Trinity, I'm not trying to be grumpy. I'm just saying I want to plan and prepare more than Grandma did," Mom responded, with a softer tone to her voice.

"I think all of us are that way, Mom, and we really don't know how long we will live," I didn't mind getting philosophical with my mom.

"That is true, as my dad did not live long at all." My mom said, looking down at the menu as though emotions were colliding in her head and I knew I needed to change the subject quickly before tears would be flowing.

"Mom, I am very proud of you," as soon as my words came out, my mom's face snapped up from looking down and focused directly on me. "You worked hard and I appreciate you always being there for me."

"Thank you, Trinity, I'm glad at least one person's proud of me," my mom replied, with her eyes getting red at the edges where tears were forming.

"Mom, the greatest thing I have learned in these last few days, being here, is that you have changed history."

My mom looked back down at the menu, pretending she was browsing through the breakfast options.

"I appreciate you saying that, Trinity. I think I have," My mom trailed off and got quiet.

"Mom, you are nothing like your dad or mom and I am nothing like you so we should celebrate with some pancakes." I praised, happy with myself for how quick I can come up with a joke to change the mood of a conversation.

My mom laughed so hard she got the attention of the waitress who came over and said she was sorry she hadn't seen us come in and sit down. Then she quickly left to get our coffees.

"The cool thing about Grandma was she was her own person. She was unique and different. That says a lot to me." I informed my mom as if she didn't know.

"Yeah, you're right Trinity, that is a good point and I forget that sometimes. Our differences were so different that sometimes I saw them as a negative thing. She was successful. She accomplished much. Unfortunately, she died a lot younger than I thought she would," my mom pointed out with a matter-of-fact tone.

"Yes, she did but what about your dad?" I answered, with a big question.

"What about him? I never really knew him well and he passed away when I was young," mom declared stirring cream into her coffee.

"Mom, I'm looking through Grandma's office and I don't really see one thing there that reminds her of him."

"What do you mean, Trin?" My mom asked, looking bewildered.

"Wouldn't you think if you were married to somebody and you had a child with them and they died, you would have pictures of them all around the house to remember them?" I said, with high hopes and expectations.

"I think she did and then when she moved from the farmhouse to this house years ago she kind of just put them away as though she were moving on to a new chapter of her life." Mom said. She assumed that was the genuine answer.

"I just don't understand how you can be married to somebody and they pass away and they die a tragic death and then you just kind of forget about them after a while," I reasoned, realizing that now I was assuming.

"I don't know, Trinity, neither of us have been through that."

"Well, you've been through a divorce," my response just came out and I was wondering how that was going to go over as it has been a sore subject in the past.

"Yes, and that is like a death but my mom didn't ask for my dad to die. I asked for a divorce."

"Why did you ask for one?" I finally had the courage to ask my mother because for so many years she only gave me quick answers on everything. Some were negative some were neutral, so I didn't really know where she stood on the entire event. In fact, I didn't even know any of the events. As I told you before, she would just say things that were just a Band-Aid of the emotions. It was almost as if she were sad or disappointed then just kind of gave a quick answer that didn't really answer anything. In fact, her quick answer only told me there are bigger answers that she hadn't told me yet. So, I guess now is a time to ask her. I didn't know how she would respond. I worried she would start talking about it and then stop as soon as the waitress got back to our booth.

"Yes, I asked for a divorce from him and at the time it was the best decision I could make for myself and for you," my mom replied, as though she was talking to an attorney and not her own daughter.

"Mom, give me the complete story." I insisted, with a slight firmness, signaling I was serious and I was tired of her quick, easy answers. Meaning, I wanted the down and dirty nitty-gritty truth about why she wanted a divorce from my biological father.

My mom exhaled with her lips turned up, blowing her bangs up as she let out all the air which I could sense was a huge breeze of frustration and almost saying I will finally get this information out. I'm going to finally tell her everything.

"Trinity, I will tell you everything then there will be no more questions," Mom said in all seriousness.

"Mom, I will always have more questions because someday I will get married and I will ask you questions. If you only answer them now, then I'm not interested. I want this to be you telling me for the first time so we can reference it as I get older."

She paused and looked at me with a soft face. Unlike any other time, I have seen her when she approaches this subject. "You are so right, Trinity," my mom said with a smile on her face. "I've been trying to keep these things back from you because I didn't think you'd understand. But I think you understand a lot more than probably I understand about it. So me telling you is probably a good thing because then we can kind of work through those painful memories together. And it probably will make it so you can understand why I've lived the way I've lived these last fifteen years or so."

"OK, Mom I am all ears."

"When I first met your dad, he was incredibly charming and made me feel really special. I took everything he said as magical. Everything he claimed I thought was real and true. I thought he really loved me. I thought he really wanted to be with me forever. I really thought he was serious about marriage and about our relationship. I mean, I told him right up front I wanted something long-term and that I wanted to be serious. I was a teenager, yet I think I was ahead of my time. I wanted something that really nobody my age who was a boy or a young man could offer me but I thought he was different. He was a little older, so I thought he was maybe more mature than people my age. We started dating and spending time together and doing many fun things. He was an artist and a sculptor and spent much of his time working on things. He didn't have much money but he was always working on the next project. So when we first started hanging out we really had a good time and it felt like it was real. We would paint or draw together. We would spend time down by the river. We would hike through the Green Mountains and look at different things. It was quite a special time." My mother kind of stared off and smiled just as the waitress returned with our breakfast.

It was almost as if my mother was glad it was a pause right there—a pause in the conversation and a way for her just to stop at that moment to remember the good times, however small they were, there were good times with my father. Stopping the conversation at this moment put everything on hold. I could tell in her mind she was back at that time enjoying the experiences she'd had with him. In fact, they had spent time in this very diner where we were now. They had conversed with each other right here, right where we're sitting. I can see why my mom would want to put it on hold for just a bit. We ate breakfast and I asked nothing more. I just wanted her to eat and enjoy the moment. The food and that she had opened up to me.

"Hey Mom." I whispered in between bites of my western omelet.

"Yes, Trin darling." My mom responded, smiling, as if it was the same time. That she knew I was about to speak.

"I'm sorry." All I said was that simple sentence.

"Honey, what are you sorry about?" My mom spoke, looking concerned for me and forgetting what we were just talking about.

"I'm sorry that he hurt you. I'm sorry that his hurt upon you changed you but I'm glad you took that negativity and made it into such a positive thing." I uttered, just barely spitting out the words as I could feel her pain.

"Trinity, how do you know he hurt me?" She went on, slightly startled that I had figured it out.

"Because I can see it in your eyes. Let's talk about this later. We can finish the story later, Mom."

"You're a smart girl and I know you know in a roundabout way what happened next but, yes, I think it's wise for us just to take a break. We can talk about it later."

I agreed and just nodded. For the rest of breakfast, my mom talked and talked and talked. She talked about memories from high school, memories of my father and she kept it right in the right place. She left it in the sweet spot. She left it right where it needed to be—the good times.

I think sometimes we put it into the negative and sometimes it belongs there but other times it doesn't. My mom kept talking over breakfast. Most of me was listening to her, though parts of me were wondering what was in that small room and my grandmother's house. I can't wait to investigate it.

I made sure to listen, though. I captured the pieces she was throwing at me. The pieces I wondered about and all those times growing up wondering if my mother was ever happy in her life. I was always wondering if she just masked all her hurt with working. She worked hard, no doubt, and she worked every day of her life. Even when she wasn't working, she was making sure that everything looked good at home and that it provided me. So I couldn't really complain but I could still ask questions. I'm thankful that I had the boldness to tell her at breakfast about her needing to tell me more details. I'm just grateful that the details she told me started off with positive ones.

That's where we are right now. That's perfect because she needs to go to the attorneys and sign papers. We are here in her hometown because her mother passed away. The fact that she is talking on and on about wonderful memories makes me incredibly satisfied.

"Do you ladies want anything else?" The waitress asked, with a smile, cutting into my mom's story.

"No thanks but the food was amazing," my mom said.

The food was amazing? I thought. The food wasn't that great at all, actually, however the conversations were. I don't think my mother tasted anything she was eating. She only tasted the memories she's so deservingly needed to consume at this moment.

My mom left a huge tip. Whoa.

Chapter 7
Raising of the Flag

As my mom drove away from the house to the attorneys, I galloped downstairs and pulled the flag down in front of the door that only I and my deceased grandmother knew about. My mother had no clue it existed. She didn't grow up in this house, so she wouldn't even know it was there. She had only been to this house a few times and never really went downstairs.

"Wait, stop for a second." I realized to myself, stopping myself right in my tracks. My mother said that my father was an artist. She didn't say he still was. Does she not know where he is right now or is he not alive? Oh great, now I've got this in my brain rattling around. I need to focus on digging through this mystery room.

When I was in this room, they're only a couple boxes and what seemed to be a cot, akin to a small bed. That's exactly what was in there, there were three boxes and they weren't labeled. You know how you label stuff when you're moving or whatever, there were three cardboard boxes I would say to be a medium size.

Curious to see what was in there, I took the first box when I turned it around and had a label on it. It was written in black marker, "bones."

"OK, bones," I thought to myself OK who keeps a box of bones in their house except for a serial killer. Which I knew my grandmother wasn't but there was that one fleeting thought going through my mind.

Opening the box that was folded shut, there were several bones inside. In fact, they had little pieces of tape taped around them that were masking tape with something written on them. They weren't huge bones, but they looked to be maybe one was a femur bone and that had tape around it that said cave behind the hill farm. OK, I thought, where is the hill farm and where is there a cave. All I could think about was when Katrina said there were some caves up on Devil's Washbowl. There was another smaller set of bones in a plastic container. Those kinds of look like chicken bones or some animal and it had written on them in what appeared to be like a sharpie marker that read "west side of road mile 2.3." I'm very confused now. This is abnormal because I've seen bone collections, but there are skeletons of animals we learned about in school you know, like my biology teacher had in her classroom.

All that was left in this box was a smaller box of bones and appeared to be some almost red color looking sand that said washbowl road east side point number one.

OK, this is so confusing. Why would my grandmother have a box of bones, they're not even labeled what animal they are? They are labeled just random things in a cave, #1 and #2. This is really confusing and I think this is just my grandmother collecting junk again.

Closing up the box, I put it right back where I found it. The second box is about the same size. Opening it up, there were clothes in there that possibly meant to be thrown away or something. They didn't look like clothes you should be saving. As I pulled them out one by one, I thought they were very interesting.

I'd been in the play and in the drama club in school, and it was almost like these were costumes or something. Obviously they must have been because normal people will not choose these things to wear. And it wasn't as if she were saving baby clothes for my mom or something. The first outfit was a pair of Capri pants that were shredded and almost tattered. Why were they folded so neatly in this box? They should have been thrown away.

Second was a pair of jeans that had a bunch of holes in them, but they were all ready and had mud on them but were folded neatly. Equally confusing.

The last was a shirt that was a red and white plaid shirt. It was a short sleeve, but it almost looked as if the sleeves were cut off to appear to be a long sleeve at one point. I'm not sure why these clothes are in this box, folded up neatly. It's almost as if it was one set of clothes for somebody.

This looks like these things are evidence from a crime or something because they're stuff we should throw away. Old bones and old clothes. This is getting unreal and like a waste of my time all at once.

The third box was a little smaller and as I opened it, I could see there's a bunch of different little things in there sliding around. At the bottom, though, were a set of boots. They're actually my size, oddly enough, but when I took them out to look at them, I noticed inside of them were huge inserts. The boots themselves had huge heels or tall heels but there was something inside of them. So I took them out of the box so they could stand up straight. Then I put the boots on and noticed how much taller I was with them on. I'm at least six to eight inches taller with these boots on. These are kind of cool actually I might want to keep these. As I put them back, I noticed that there was a small clear plastic box that had several fake nails in there with glue. I knew they were fake nails. I've had them before several times and when I used to play dress up when I was younger I used to put them on a lot more frequently.

Below them in this box was a grocery bag plastic one that had three wigs in it. When I took them out, they were so creepy looking. The three wigs had shorter hair. I'm almost like spiked hair, it was so short and they were the dirty blonde or light brown hair; different from my hair. Mine is long and black and these are short and light brown. I definitely have no use for them, I said, laughing aloud.

I just find it strange that my grandmother had these items in this closet underneath the stairs. It just makes little sense. If you're going to hide anything cool in here, you might hide money or something that was valuable. None of the stuff seems worth anything. Who wants an old army cot? It smells so musty in here. Well, that was kind of letdown and I was hoping to find more treasure in there.

I better get upstairs to throw things away from the top rooms. My mother had already made some big piles and she wanted me to throw those away in the dumpster. As I walked up the stairs, I got a text from Katrina.

Hey Trinity, it's Katrina. When you get a second can we FaceTime? I have some things that might be of interest to you.

I texted right back, absolutely let's talk I'm getting bored and I don't feel like moving a bunch of boxes out to the trash.

Hey, Trinity, thank you for FaceTiming. It's good to see you. How are things going with you?

As you can see the mess behind me, I have a lot to do today and I'm really bored already.

Listen to this, I was looking through some of my grandmother's stuff and I found something that you might be interested in. Katrina wrote as if she were a detective.

Definitely if it's a typewriter or something cool or worth a lot, I'm definitely interested. I inserted it to lighten the mood.

Let me hold the document up to the camera on the phone so you can see it.

OK, I see it, explain it to me it is. It looks like a medical document, or even like a bill or something. Does my grandmother owe a medical bill?

No, it's a statement from a doctor and at the beginning it is for the salutation or whatever you call the beginning of a letter, it's to both of our grandmothers.

Why is that weird, Katrina, they're both been on the same historical committee for years?

Yah, I know that, but read further. Katrina instructed with a sense of eagerness.

I can't read it, Katrina, as the font is too small. Plus, you're moving around too much and it's grainy. The internet here isn't working well.

OK, I will take a pic of it and text it to you right now. Katrina quickly snapped a pic and sent it off.

Excellent, thank you, here it is. I read it aloud to Katrina.

Dear Linda and Bobby Jo,

I appreciate you bringing me the DNA samples of what you retrieved at the historical site. I say historical site, meaning that much has taken place in those areas you have defined. I tested the DNA samples in the laboratory and

they are not like anything I've ever seen before. In fact, they have DNA I've never really seen combined in any human before at all. Of course, you know that DNA testing is in its early stages and is not 100 percent accurate right now. I hope it will get better as the years go on.

I know you have contact with the person we are discussing, and I hope they are seeking help for the issues that they are facing.

I am including a printout of the DNA coding that was produced by our computers.

I do believe and strongly suggest that this matter from here on out be handled by the Federal Bureau of Investigation. I feel this is a national issue, especially for mutations and humans and the study of DNA. I know no crime has taken place but when it comes to changes in the DNA of humans, the more people who know about it, the better.

Thank you again for reaching out to me. I appreciate all your information and I enjoyed talking to the two of you. Please keep me posted with any additional news.
Sincerely
James F. Harrison, MD.
Boston Foundation for DNA Research"

That is bizarre. I replied slowly, still examining the letter.

It definitely freaked me out, Trinity, so I wanted to contact you immediately because I've never heard of anything like this.

My grandmother never talked about this either and I'm not sure what they're talking about. I was still in shock.

I immediately thought of the Pigman. Trinity, that's why I contacted you.

Wait a second, what is the date on that letter? I addressed Katrina as there was a light going off in my brain.

It is from about 20 years ago. Why do you ask?

Under my grandmother's stairs is a room that was hidden and inside it there boxes and I noticed each of them were marked, October 2000.

Yeah, that is strange because this letter postmarked November 2000.

That is peculiar because what I found in the boxes were human clothes, fake fingernails and wigs just to name a few things. I listed off the findings.

That is more than strange. Katrina added.

Katrina, I think it's time that we pay a visit to the library.

To the library. Why would we want to go there? I wondered, because I wasn't really known for wanting to go to the library.

I find it strange that in my grandmother's office there isn't much about the Pigman at all. Yet, in this room that's hidden are these random pieces. There's actually a box of bones. I almost left out the eeriest part.

Bones? All I can think of is the bones they found in different places that belong to the

Pigman's animals he ate that he had stolen from the local farms.

Oh my goodness, you're right, I never thought of that. I forgot you had talked about that on our walk to Devil's Washbowl.

This is getting deeper into crazy by the second. Why do you want to go to the library though? I asked.

We need to find every article that has to do with a Pigman. I know there must be some in this house and my grandmother's but I don't know where they are and how to even go about finding them. I don't even know if my mother's already thrown them out." Katrina replied, frantically.

So what do you think we can accomplish at the library? I asked, not knowing what Katrina was thinking.

They have those machines that we can look through old newspapers. Plus, we can print them out right there. Because I know not all of them are on the internet, some of them are just stored at the library itself and you know how the technology is around here.

I do, it is frustrating. So let's meet there tomorrow morning because it's already closed by now. I informed her.

Let me do some more searching here at home then we will meet in the morning and get a game plan together. Katrina advised as if she had been organizing these types of things her whole life.

I will do the same here. If I find any articles over here at my grandma's house about the Pigman, I will bring them in the morning. I added. Also, we need to investigate this letter. Who is this doctor and this place in Boston?

Yes. I will work on it. Katrina agreed.

That sounds like a plan, Katrina, and thank you for texting and FaceTiming. I wasn't sure why I was thanking her but I was sure glad that she was interested. Like me.

I am thankful you are here. You are making this town look exciting for once. Katrina commented as she smiled into her phone. Except for the Pigman.

Yes, I replied, laughing. Exciting and I look forward to seeing you.

After she hung up something just hit me. *Wait a second*, I thought, *Katrina's mom is the librarian and they're moving a lot of my grandmother's stuff to the library. I know my mom will not be thrilled that I'm going to the library to look up the Pigman. I've got to figure out a reason to get me to the library without causing a lot of commotion.*

Just then, my mom pulled in the driveway and she still looked happy even though she had just met with the attorney for several hours. She was probably still happy from our breakfast and the time we had there.

As my mom walked in, she had an entire stack of papers in several envelopes

"How do things go for you today, Ms. Trinity?" She asked, looking around at all that was left to do.

"I took care of both of those piles you had in the front bedroom and threw everything away in the dumpster," I reported to my mom.

"That is awesome. I am so glad we're making progress. I signed a bunch of papers today and I officially own the house so we can get this thing cleaned out and sold." My mom exhaled with a smile of relief.

"That sounds like a good idea to me. Katrina and I talk today and we will spend some time together tomorrow. Is that OK with you?" I asked quickly, hoping to get the answer I wanted.

"Sounds like a great idea. I think you'll need a break from all this. I don't mean to put all of this on you, Trin. I remember being fourteen. It wasn't always so fun." She said, which I was surprised to hear.

"I absolutely do. I'm glad though that you seem to be having a good day today. Yes, mom, I have seen pictures of you when you were fourteen. You definitely aren't as cool as I am." Joking with her as she was always reluctant to show me pictures of her going through adolescence.

"Hey, I am cool now," my mom expressed with light-hearted giggles. "Yeah, the attorneys were a little stressful but I think it'll be good to sell this home and use that money to invest and save for your college, which is not far away."

"I know. The more and more I spend time here and look through Grandma's stuff, the more I want to be a writer or an editor." I confirmed with a level of excitement, though I wasn't sure if I was just excited because of the whole Pigman thing.

"That sounds wonderful, and Pennsylvania has a ton of cool colleges right near where we live." Mom informed me as if I didn't know that information already.

"Yes, that is a brilliant plan, Mom, and how about we order some subs for dinner? I'm hungry and I don't see a lot of food around this house." I said, knowing my mom would instantly accept such an awesome idea of mine.

My mom laughed and agreed as she reached for the phone to call for a takeout order

"Mom, I hope dinner is just as good as breakfast was," putting my hand on her shoulder.

My mom smiled again.

Chapter 8
In the News

"OK, Mom, Katrina is here, I said, getting her attention. Mom is already knee deep in piles. She still seemed happy, though. She was sad her mother was gone and I was sad my grandmother was not with us anymore. I think my mom was forming an appreciation for her, which made me happy too.

"You two have fun this morning," my mom cheered among the mess that was, oddly enough, getting smaller.

"We are going to the diner first for breakfast," I confirmed, knowing she would want to go with us but couldn't.

"Great idea," mom agreed with an envious smile. Take your time and enjoy your day, Trin."

"Thanks Mom, see you soon," I assured her as I shut the door behind me.

As I walked out, I could see that Katrina was all business. Her backpack looked filled, as if she was going to school.

When we sat down at the diner the same waitress came over who had served my mother and I.

"What can I get you two this morning?" The waitress inquired with a bubbly disposition.

"Just coffee for me," Katrina clarified, as if it were a business meeting.

"I will have the western omelet with white toast and, also, I would like a large orange juice," I ordered, knowing I would use my brain, and that always makes me hungry.

"I've been doing some investigation," Katrina reported, looking at me as she was pulling a notebook out of her book bag.

"OK, what do you have?" I inquired, eagerly.

"Trinity, I looked up that Doctor from our grandmother's letter. I want to show you this article. I was here yesterday evening while my mother was closing up the library and I printed this out for you. Read the part that I highlighted. It's just from a couple years ago."

I read aloud, "Doctor claims on his deathbed, he personally saw a mutated man that looks like he was half pig. Skeptics and his family close to him contributed to part of his dementia."

"This is the doctor from that letter, Trinity."

"I'm confused. Did this doctor see the Pigman? Or was it just part of a DNA test? I am not understanding this at all."

"Yes, it puts a wrench in our gears already and we haven't even started researching. We need to find as many articles as we can. So let's search under Pigman or half pig half man," Katrina suggested.

"I agree and we'll print out everything so we have it." I said, trying to be organized. "The only thing is we need the actual newspaper or Facebook articles and not just people's opinion because many people don't believe in it and many people believe in it so how are we going to get an impartial point of view?"

"I think my mom will help us get the articles because she can just as easily access them and print them out and then we can look through them. I think it would be fun too, maybe even start a story about this and kind of resurrect it," Katrina said it all to me in one breath.

"I'm definitely all for that but I just kind of want the truth. It's like people believe it or they don't but are they looking for factual information or are they just looking for the emotions of it? Because when something's scary it's cool but let's say, if it's not even real is it still scary."

"Trinity, that is a brilliant point and I see what you're saying. I think it would be good for us just to get the points of view that have been stated and are only aligned with facts." Katrina said, diplomatically.

"Yeah, good poin,." even though I was kind of getting confused. I just wanted answers.

"My mom will let us use the back room where there's a gigantic table so we can put everything, kind of like on a timeline or something."

"Brilliant idea, Katrina," I was speaking as though we had been a team for years.

"But, I want you to first look at this article. It actually made the New York Times and other major newspapers and was all over social media. It seems a little surreal to me."

Katrina took a printed article and placed it on the table.

Downstate New York woman Chased, Harassed and Assaulted by the Pigman of Northfield Vermont

Brenda Waverly of Poughkeepsie, New York, was on a leisure vacation in the Green mountains of Northfield, Vermont. She was sightseeing in the spot called Devil's Washbowl when she was brutally attacked by what appeared to be a Pigman. "I could see it running down through the field and then I noticed it was coming toward me so I turned and ran to get back to my car. It was squealing and was making all sorts of weird sounds. I was petrified." Mrs. Waverly was then assaulted by the Pigman as she tried to enter her car to get to safety. Her injuries were treated at a local hospital. "It was the worst experience in my life. I never knew that such a human existed. I was just minding my own business and it came out of nowhere." Mrs. Waverly was treated for her injuries and released shortly afterward.

"Why is this out of norm, Katrina? It went national, it went viral, how cool is that."

"It's wonderful but it's the only article that went national and it's the only name I don't recognize," Katrina confessed softly. Almost as if she was worried somebody was listening.

"I'm not understanding what you mean by a name you don't recognize."

"Trinity, every article is local and I know the people. They still live around here. They're easy to talk to and they've told their story many times; but this woman in this article I've never heard of and her story hasn't ever been referenced by my grandmother or your grandmother." Katrina informed me.

"OK, so what should we do?" I wasn't sure what she was getting at but it seemed odd to me that this was the one article that went national.

"We need to contact her," Katrina stated, while I looked intently at her, "she runs a yoga studio in downstate New York."

"You mean contact her to interview her about the Pigman? Why?" I asked, wondering how this was a good idea.

"We will tell her we're doing a new story on the Pigman for the Northfield historian. That is kind of true." Katrina offered, trying to get me on board with the idea.

"Even more brilliant idea," I proclaimed exuberantly. "Count me in. This sounds like a great idea. I would like to get her viewpoint on all this. This town is even more interesting," I said, smiling.

We need not go to the library. We need to make two phone calls.

"Before we make the phone calls, I need to show you some pictures I took of what I found in my grandmother's house." I said, opening my backpack.

"What?" Katrina asked as she stopped and turned toward me.

"Yes, it is a secret room below the stairs."

Chapter 9

Making the Call

"We can call her at her Yoga business," Katrina suggested.

"So are you going to call?" I asked nervously, knowing what the answer would be.

"I am not good at stuff like that," Katrina admitted. I was wondering when she had ever done something like knowing that she wasn't good at it.

I called her. On speakerphone so that Katrina could listen in and take notes.

"Good afternoon, am I speaking to Holly Wilson?" I asked nervously and wondered if she would think I was a telemarketer.

"Yes, it is," she answered jubilantly.

"Well, my name is Trinity Porter and we are doing a news story about the Pigman of Northfield, Vermont, and wanted to get your version of what your experience with it was like?" I asked, trying to sound like a reporter and not an obsessed high schooler. Katrina smiled and gave a thumbs up sign.

"I remember going to Northfield and spending a few days there. I was there as I was teaching yoga to some local people. In fact, it was in a group of some older ladies in the community. My friends and I go on a vacation every year together. Ever since we graduated from college. In that year we decided as a group to take a trip up to Vermont. We found a nice house we could rent up in Northfield. So we went. We were out for breakfast at this diner and some local ladies who were talking about needing a yoga instructor in the area. I told them I could help them and teach them some poses and routines," she explained.

"Holly, where were you when you first spotted the Pigman?" I asked, trying to get Holly to the juicy parts of the story.

"I never did," Holly uttered in what sounded to be the shortest sentence.

"I am confused, as according to the news article, you had a run-in with him," I recalled, explaining her own story to her.

"No, not at all. Many people called me and asked me about it and I was very confused. Yes, I was in the town but never saw a Pigman. They certainly talked about him but I never saw him. I never claimed to have seen him, so I'm very confused by all this," Holly explained in a calm voice.

"Do you remember the group of ladies that you taught yoga to?" I asked, not sure why I had asked except for the hope that she was kidding us.

"Well, let me think, one of the ladies was the town historian or something like that. She was a very interesting older lady. I believe her name was Linda. With her was another woman who was her friend. I can't remember her first name. Her last name I think started with a T, gosh it's been a few years," she sighed, trying to recall.

"Was it Tallman?" I asked, as Katrina's face looked concerned.

"Yes, that's it. We had a wonderful time and they were very interesting ladies. We never made it back up there as we thought we were going to. I have actually never seen the new article. I just figured it was a typo." She explained in a boring way.

"I'm sorry to have bothered you, Mrs. Wilson. I'm not sure why this article was printed with your name on it." I said, trying to explain all the confusion.

"I could never figure out who wrote the article either but that's OK, it doesn't bother me. There's no harm done. I just always figured there was a misprint all these years." Holly said, as if it didn't bother her at all.

"I think you're right,'' I agreed. Thanks again for your time.

Ending the call, Katrina just stared at me. "Well, that was an interesting phone call, Trinity. Not only interesting, but disturbing."

"Yes, this plot is starting to get extremely thick," I stressed, as we looked down at the pile of paperwork we had been accumulating.

"We need to call the doctor's widow." Katrina suggested rereading her grandmother's letter she had found.

"We should just call your grandmother and ask her." I suggested, thinking it would shed more light on the questions we had.

"No way," Katrina sputtered, with an increase in her volume. "She will freak out. Here is the phone number for Dr. Harrison's wife, Milley," she said, changing the subject and assuming I was going to make all the phone calls.

"It is going into voicemail," I stated, though we both could hear. "I will leave a voicemail. Maybe she will call back."

"Good idea," Katrina agreed.

"Good afternoon Mrs. Harrison, my name is Trinity Porter and I am doing a new story in Northfield, Vermont, about the Pigman and wanted to ask you a couple of questions. Thank you." I said, trying to sound both friendly and professional.

"I hope she calls back, Trinity. I am so nervous," Katrina cautioned.

"What are you worried for? She has my name and phone number, not yours," I reminded her.

"While we wait, let's get busy reading the rest of these articles I printed out." Katrina suggested, pulling a thick folder filled with papers.

Chapter 10
Prom Invite

"Let's go to my grandmother's house and I will show you the little room below the stairs. It was locked and covered with a flag, so I know it was to be not seen by my mom." I suggested, knowing Katrina would be up for the adventure.

As we started to walk back to my grandmother's house there was an older woman walking down the sidewalk. She stopped in front of us as she was obviously familiar with Katrina.

"Hi Katrina, how are you and your family doing?" she asked with a lot of high energy.

"Everybody's doing well, Mrs. Ackerman." Katrina spoke politely.

"What are you two young ladies up to?" Mrs. Ackerman asked, thinking it was none of her business.

"We're just doing some research on the Pigman, actually," Katrina announced, as I looked puzzled at her, thinking *why would she tell her what we were doing.*

"Hey," I interrupted, elbowing Katrina in the side and whispering, "What are you doing? Why are you telling her?"

"You'll see," Katrina turned and winked at me.

"Oh, I know all too much about the Pigman. I'll never forget what he looked like in the bushes. He was making strange squealing sounds and a real small kind of human-like creature." She boasted, looking at both of us in the eyes.

"Mrs. Ackerman, you're saying it had a high pitch squeal?" Katrina asked.

"Yes, very high pitched, almost like a little kid screaming." Mrs. Ackerman scowled.

"Oh, I forgot to introduce you to my friend, Trinity, who is Linda Porter's granddaughter." Katrina exclaimed, pointing to me.

"I'm so sorry to hear about your loss. She and I went to school together and we graduated together." Mrs. Ackerman fretted with sad eyes.

"I appreciate you saying that, Mrs. Ackerman, and so you were saying you went to school with my grandmother?" I asked, trying to sound interested.

"Yes I did, we went all the way through school together and graduated from high school. We both have lived in this town since we were born." Mrs. Ackerman explained.

I had an ah-ha moment, "So if she was in the same class as you, was she at the dance that night?"

"Actually, I remember for a fact that she didn't go. I was not happy because I knew the dance would be boring unless your grandmother was there. I do remember your grandmother, Katrina, was the one outside yelling she was seeing something. I remember because I was sitting alone at the table with my date and was wishing Linda would have been there. Katrina, your grandmother got up to use the restroom. We couldn't hear much as we were seated up by the stage and the band was a little loud. Then we all heard her scream. I would have too, as she had seen the creature that would be famously called the Pigman," Mrs. Ackerman recalled. "Oh, I have to run, I am late to the dentist. You girls enjoy your day."

"Yes, that is very interesting, Mrs. Ackerman, and thank you for sharing. We have to go now too," Katrina interjected, as we started walking away.

We walked away. It only took a few steps and I stopped and turned and looked in Katrina's eyes. She looked at me, wondering why I was staring at her.

"Katrina, she said something very strange." I declared, squinting deep into her eyes. "It is mysterious that my grandmother was not at her own senior prom and your grandmother was the one who discovered the Pigman."

"Good point, Trinity, that is unusual." Katrina agreed, looking mystified herself.

"There are so many layers to this now. I'm getting confused," I freely admitted. "Let's walk by the old high school and look at a couple of things."

"The high school is now a bunch of apartments, so I am not sure what is the purpose of going there, Trinity?" Katrina asked.

Walking down a side street, we arrived at the back of the old high school.

"Katrina, look at where the gymnasium is and where the back door is that your grandmother went out and saw the Pigman and screamed." I said, pointing at the back areas.

"Yeah. So." Katrina echoed, speaking as I do sometimes to my mother, for which I get in trouble.

"She was going to the bathroom, as Mrs. Ackerman stated. That is near the stage and out the doors in the school area. Why would she go out the back door of the gymnasium or even walk by the back door on the way to the bathrooms? They are located at the complete opposite end." I listed, ordering the events as best as I could from all the different pieces of information I had.

"Whoa. You just gave me goosebumps," Katrina replied, with a sense of fear in her voice.

"Plus, Mrs. Ackerman said they were surprised to hear her screaming as she was up by the stage where the band was. That also proves they weren't sitting anywhere near the back doors of the gymnasium." I added.

"This is beyond messed up, Trinity. This town has been lied to all these years? Or is it real? I am beyond confused," Katrina sputtered. She was starting to get emotional.

“Let’s not worry yet. We have more work to do.” I assured her, trying to reassure Katrina as she was visibly upset.

“So what about the doctor’s letter? Was that real too? Katrina asked with such fear in her eyes and voice. She was quickly unraveling.

“Let’s go look at the secret room and take a brief break,” I suggested.

“I think I want to go home now. I am feeling kind of sick,” Katrina gulped, looking a little flush in her skin.

“I don’t blame you,” I supported her statement, “I am tired from all this thinking.”

Chapter 11

What a Picture is Worth

When I got back to my grandmother's home, my mother was on the couch taking a nap. I went back down to the writing room and continued to look for things.

There must be something else down here, I thought. *There's just got to be something more to help us figure out what is the truth here.*

There were two boxes I hadn't gone through and I started going through a box with what looked to be just a bunch of papers. It looked as if my grandmother had taken the mail each day, looked through the bills and then put the junk mail in this pile.

Going down through the box, I could see it was mostly junk mail that hadn't even been opened. There were some bills thrown in there and some old newspapers.

I went to pick up the pile and throw it back in the box. There was a photo that slid out and onto the floor. It was what appeared to be a police sketch of a man that looked to be a Pigman.

At the bottom of the photo it was stamped in red, "Police Evidence Case#: VT 1852571."

When I turned it over, it read, "your resemblance is uncanny."

I quickly put it in a large envelope I found on my grandmother's desk. I sealed it and put it into my backpack.

This was just another big question mark for me. The more I learned, the less I understood the big picture.

I needed to readjust my thinking. This was fascinating and I love to write, so it was an interesting plot with many twists and turns. I was sad my grandmother was gone, though I was excited about what she had left me.

I could hear my mom waking up.

Was the Pigman really a deformed human? Was it all about it being a demonic creature? Was this a genetic experiment that had gone horribly wrong? Was this just my grandmother all along?

Did Urma Applebaum, my grandmother, create the actual plot in her life so it would be authentic enough to sell on paper.

Should I call the police or the newspapers? Or do I say nothing at all? And leave it as it is. I don't know which tradition should be carried on or kept hidden away forever. Could I play the part? Where are the ethics in all this? Should I tell my mother?

I don't know whether to throw rocks at the framed pictures or to frame them in gold. She was either a cold, heartless person or a genius. Did she create a monster or a fairy tale that brought a town closer together? Really, she put this town on the map and herself.

My mom came downstairs as I snapped out of my thought fog.

"You threw away a lot of boxes, I see." Mom affirmed, visibly exhausted from her nap.

"Yes, and I kept a few."

"There is something I need to ask you?" Mom asked as I froze, thinking she had seen the secret room.

"What is that, Mom?" I asked, looking out the window.

"I need to come back here this summer. I have vacation time. I know it is boring here, so I just might come back by myself. You can go stay with Gina, I already talked to her mom. She said it was OK. Then you don't have to be far from home," Mom uttered, almost apologetically.

"Oh, Mom, I don't mind," I asserted, quickly.

"You sure, honey, as it is so boring here and this has been not much fun for you." Mom assumed, not knowing the truth, "but I am seeing the positive impact Grandma had here. She is really missed by all of us."

I froze. I was unaware of so many feelings, words and history my mother had, plus, the ones I had discovered. I guess we both had unearthed quite a bit.

"Don't worry, Mom, I am sure there will be a lot going on here this summer. I can just feel it."

That's all I can tell you about my problem.

Wait a second, I forgot. We came here a few years ago around Halloween. My aunt had passed when I was ten or eleven. It was my father's only living relative. That year I think Halloween was on a Saturday, so we stayed for the weekend and went trick-or-treating. As I remember, the funeral was on a Friday and we stayed until Sunday.

I went and found my mom. She was lugging a box to the dining room that looked like it might have some water damage on it.

"Mom, do you have any pics from when we were here for Halloween?" I asked if I really needed the answer.

"I remember that was when Aunt Judy died. Yeah, I think I have some here in my camera roll somewhere on my phone." Mom said, as she started scrolling through her phone. She stopped and looked up. "Trinity, all I remember is actually me and Grandma getting into a heated argument."

"Why," I asked inquisitively, trying not to sound as if I didn't know they fought a lot. In light of her passing, I didn't want to be or sound rude.

"She knew I wanted to take you trick or treating and I thought it would be a good time for the three of us to spend some time together. She was telling me she had a meeting that night and she did not like Halloween at all. In fact, that ended up being a night where there was a Pigman sighting, I believe." My mom said, trying to recall the events with some respect towards her.

Growing increasingly excited I asked, "Pigman sighting?"

"Yeah, there was a Pigman sighting up in the typical areas where they see them and then she had to go investigate after she got back from her meeting. We never really saw anything that night but you and I had a good time. We went through the entire town and got a bunch of candy then we ended up going to…"

"Oh yeah, the firehouse," I interrupted. I remember now, we went down there and played games and it was a lot of fun. I guess we didn't really need grandmother to have fun." I said to make my mom feel better. I could tell she was feeling yucky about everything.

"Yes, and I didn't want it to be about her and I arguing so we kept it very quiet but I remembered her not being there for us too and that bothered me," My mom said in a monotone, as if she were reliving the moment in a more calm tone.

"Oh, here it is," My mom laughed as she showed me a picture of that Halloween.

"What's so funny I asked, walking closer and taking her phone from her hand so I could zoom in. "Here is the picture of you and me and you are dressed up like Harry Potter," she said, changing her laughter into a frozen smile.

"Ugh," I replied, "those were some awkward times for sure."

We both laughed. Which, as you know, isn't a common occurrence.

"Mom, if we came here for Halloween, did we come back for Christmas?" I asked gently to not look as if I were digging slightly for dirt.

"Yes, we did, but Mom was busy from Halloween onto the Christmas season because of those ridiculous Pigman sightings."

Playing ignorant to everything, "Pigman sightings? Why would that make her busy?" I asked.

"Trin, she was busy doing those tours, those foolish Pigman tours where people believe that stuff. She was busy all the way to Christmas and even beyond." Mom paused. "You know as I think about it, Trinity, it's almost as if there was a sighting every Halloween and, as you know, your grandmother never liked Halloween, anyway, so this kept her busy, that's for sure."

"Mom, when you were young, did she like Halloween?" I asked diplomatically.

"No, she really didn't." My mom said sadly, "this whole Pigman thing made me miss out on a lot of things and I didn't want that to happen to you so I made it known to her if we were going to come here for Christmas she had better be available or we weren't going to bother." My mom said, recalling the emotions she felt during that time. "But anyway," my mom continued with a softer tone, "I am relieved that is in the past and we do need to be thankful for all your grandmother was because she was obviously a big part of this community and she is missed by all of us."

"Yeah," I agreed, contemplating all that was said. "I do miss her a lot and I wish I could just talk to her for one more time. Me and her. To just sit down and converse with her before she had to leave, as I have so many questions for her." I said, with a heavy heart and the beginnings of tears.

"Yes Trinity, I can see why you would want that and I do wish I could have said goodbye to her, as well. I do love and miss her and I do wish she were back. She would be very proud of you, Trinity, for all you're doing and how you're helping with her house," Mom declared as if she wanted to divert the attention from her to me, acting as if she were starting to cry.

"Mom," I paused, as I could feel emotions coming on me as a bat about to strike a ball. "I'm sure she's proud of you as you've done so much in life and accomplished much. I think it's pretty cool how we're here right now and we are enjoying our time here. That is a rarity." I said, not knowing what the response would be.

"Good point, Trinity, I was dreading to come here but, when I started to go through all that fills this house and there are quite few memories I've forgotten. Positive memories." She said, with some closure in her voice.

Epilogue

So that's, my story. This is where I am right now in my life. Summer, will be here soon.

The saddest part is my grandmother passed away. I will miss her every day. She was a lot like me and I'm thankful that my mother appreciates her.

I'm also grateful my mother has changed from the passing of her mother. Death changes us. When someone is close to us, their passing changes us in so many ways. We reflect more about life and its meaning. My mother is doing that right now. So am I.

She almost seems to have some type of revival that she's come back to where she grew up.

She's seeing memories as fond and to be cherished. I am glad she is happy. Even if it's for a moment, she is happy being back where she started her life; where she went to elementary school, where she graduated from high school. We drove by the sports fields where she played soccer and softball. She had many stories, of which I am always interested in hearing.

Typically, she is tight-lipped. She even opened up about my father. Talking to me about what happened and why it didn't work out. She seems to be more free.

With all this going on, though, there is a bigger story behind the scenes. An entire town here is afraid of the Pigman. There are many stories and legends that have kept this town alive with intrigue and some fear.

As the Robert Frost poem says, two roads diverged in the wood. My question is, which road do I take?

(My mom has mentioned frequently that Robert Frost lived somewhere near where she grew up.)

The Road Not Taken
by Robert Frost
Two roads diverged in a yellow wood,
And sorry I could not travel both
And be one traveler, long I stood
And looked down one as far as I could
To where it bent in the undergrowth;

Then took the other, as just as fair,
And having perhaps the better claim,

Because it was grassy and wanted wear;
Though as for that the passing there
Had worn them really about the same,

And both that morning equally lay
In leaves no step had trodden black.
Oh, I kept the first for another day!
Yet knowing how way leads on to way,
I doubted if I should ever come back.
I shall be telling this with a sigh
Somewhere ages and ages hence:
Two roads diverged in a wood, and I—
I took the one less traveled by,
And that has made all the difference.

What road would you take? I thought. When you're getting ready to get out of middle school, all you're focused on is high school. I haven't even given it a thought—not concerned about high school, right now. I know I'm going into the ninth grade. That is obvious, at least. I am excited eighth grade is almost over but a lot has only just begun.

I only have a few weeks to make my decisions. As soon as school is out, we are heading right back up to my grandmother's home. I already agreed to stay there the whole summer. My mother was very excited about it, too. So, I don't have a lot of time but I have a lot to process and think about.

I know Katrina will wait for me. She talks about it every day. She is constantly doing research and is texting me about it.

Katrina's mom found out what we are doing, that we are researching the Pigman. She only knows the part that we're just doing it for the fun of it but she has been an immense help. She has given Katrina many articles. Also, Katrina has talked to several locals and listened to their side of the story. She has recorded them. She sends me the recordings so I can listen to them. Some of them, I think, are legit, others I'm not so sure of, at this point.

I don't know what to believe and that is one of the worst feelings in the world.

What I know and don't know is:

The facts are:

- We have a doctor's widow who hasn't called us back. What does she know? Is she even still alive?
- We have a woman who they made a whole fake news article about, which caused the locals to be even more scared. Who wrote the article? How was it put into the newspaper?
- I have a secret room in my grandmother's home with all the stuff in there having to do with Pigman. Why did my grandmother have that room? What was she hiding?
- We looked at the layout of the high school prom and it makes little sense that Mrs. Tallman would walk by the back doors of the gymnasium. Also, my grandmother wasn't at the dance.
- Then there was the police composite drawing of the Pigman with the message on the back.

Katrina just texted that she has some news that is bigger than the news we have. I'm not sure what that means but I will find out soon. She wants me to call her in about an hour.

Watch for the sequel to *Urma Applebaum and the Pigman.*

Will Trinity find out more about the Pigman or will she actually see the Pigman?

About the Author

Damon Piletz (Rich Unkel) is an enrichment teacher, private investigator, and adjunct college professor. As a native New Englander, he has always been fascinated with unsolved mysteries and eager to learn of the different legends that were talked about in many small towns. The Pigman of Northfield, Vermont being one of them.

Equipped with a wide range of experiences, Damon uses them to teach students from preschool to graduate level. In addition to three published books, he has had several poems and short stories featured in various literary publications. After residing in New York for several years, Damon returned to New England and lives in Vermont with his family.

www.ingramcontent.com/pod-product-compliance
Ingram Content Group UK Ltd.
Pitfield, Milton Keynes, MK11 3LW, UK
UKHW021050270726
13967UKWH00012B/192

9 780692 203514